BOOK ONE
THE SECOND COMING

CHAPTER ONE
BROKEN EGGS CAN BE MENDED

Like the banner of an empire exhausted, an American flag hung limp on its pole, a winked-out razzmatazz of guttered stars and strangled stripes. The Red, White and Blue had faded to Pink, Gray and Livid.

The morning clouds were fat with rain.

A leaf stirred, and dirt moved. The ground rumbled.

Then the wind howled out of the prairie like a freight train barreling down the tracks.

The flag leapt alert, and snapped to attention. Old Glory, stars ablaze, was new again, back in bold primary colors. Flapping furiously, the flag strained at the bridle of its rope, which was as taut as a bowstring drawn back by an invisible hand. For a moment the wind achieved gale-force intensity, and then slackened and died. Through a widening rent in the clouds a radiant shaft of sunlight shone down on a tomb near the flagpole. An obelisk more than a hundred feet tall presided over the gravesite. In the catacombs underground was a red marble cenotaph. The date was April 15, 2015, the sesquicentennial of the death of Abraham Lincoln. The cenotaph cracked apart as the ground underneath it opened with a roar.

From that chasm a rangy, black-clad man crawled out. He was as long as a beanpole, and as ugly as a scarecrow. On reaching the floor he swatted dirt from his suit, which was stiffened with age and grime and resembled the attire of a superannuated undertaker. He sought for his watch attached to a gold chain that led to a fob in his vest, and was puzzled not to find it. He looked around. His head was mainly a skull but already the flesh was regrowing as were his whiskers, which blossomed anew into a full beard. He was holding a stovepipe hat full of squirming maggots. He looked it over for a few moments, swatted dirt off of it and then turned it over to expel the vermin, which landed on the floor with a sickening plop. A scrap of paper from one of his long-lost speeches drifted down from the overturned hat and alighted on the writhing pestilence. He then planted the hat atop his head but not before, unknown to him, a sparrow alighted in the bird's nest of his hair. He reached into his coat pockets, took out two handfuls of worms and hurled them to the floor, too. Turning to his left, he saw the following words engraved upon a wall near the ceiling: "Now he belongs to the ages." The man pondered this for a few moments and then said in a reedy, piping voice: "Well, I'd rather the ages belonged to me. And I reckon I'm pretty aged, so I guess they do." He loped out into the Illinois dawn, this cadaverous old rail splitter did. Back at last: beating Christ to the punch by some two thousand years.

Alternatively, in the depths of night in what might have been a black-box, black-book, Black Ops project — or not — black-clad figures shimmied down rope ladders from hovering black helicopters and, armed with pick axes, hammers, Soviet-era Kalashnikov rifles and sticks of dynamite, blasted their way into the cenotaph and dragged out the gangling corpse by its long legs ... shouting "Allahu Akbar," perhaps, or perhaps not. At this point, as in a

Abe 2.0: Welcome to the Asylum, Mr. President
Copyright © 2016 David M.

Printed in the Asylum, and the United States of America

ISBN-10: 1-944854-01-0
ISBN-13: 978-1-944854-01-0

Publisher
Pood Paw Prints LLC
https://www.poodpawprints.com
https://www.facebook.com/poodpawprints
Press information: thorson@poodpawprints.com

Production Editor
David M

Cover Art
Scott Thorson

Other books from Pood Paw Prints
The Pood: Michigan's Inferno

ABE 2.0
A NOVELLA IN TWO BOOKS

BOOK ONE: THE SECOND COMING

BOOK TWO: THE FATEFUL LIGHTNING

Gogol tale, everything becomes befogged ...

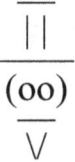

A squad car pulled out of the parking lot of a Dunkin' Donuts outlet in Springfield, and turned onto East Lawrence Avenue. It was ten in the morning, the sky as blue as eyes.

At the wheel was Sergeant Sullivan (Sully) Stark.

"The clouds cleared up in a jiffy," he remarked, peering out the windshield and up at the sky. "Never seen anything like that. Seemed like a giant fan blew 'em away."

He reached into the bag of donuts on the seat between him and his partner and fished out one of his favorites, covered in chocolate. He took a bite, and then set the donut on a napkin on the dashboard.

"Pure death," his partner, Rob Boyle, announced, staring at the black donut as if it were a black suspect. "Stroke City, Sergeant. If you don't mind my saying."

"Mmm! Donuts!" Stark said jocularly. He reached for the lidless Styrofoam cup of coffee in a holder between their seats, sipped the bitter brew, judged it insufficiently sweet and then set it back down.

Boyle, twenty-five years old, was a rookie, as green as a string bean. Sergeant Stark's gaze wandered down to his own sprawling paunch, in contrast to Boyle's washboard belly. The sergeant was fifty-five years old and looking forward to early retirement.

"Have one," Stark said, offering the bag of donuts to Boyle.

Boyle grimaced. Stark set the bag down again.

Glancing up at the rear-view mirror, Stark saw a

stranger's eyes staring back at him.

They were bloodshot and defeated and set in the sagging purple pouches of a gloomy basset-hound face. He wondered: *Who is that?*

Then he recognized himself.

He sighed.

Their shift had just started, but already Stark was looking forward to returning home to his racetrack totes and to his decomposing wife, Hortense, who was cared for by a live-in nurse from Haiti. The nurse was long-suffering and infinitely forbearing: a stoic bearer of crosses.

"And how is Mrs. Stark, Sergeant Stark?" Boyle asked out of the blue, in a strangely chipper tone of voice.

Alzheimer, flashed through Stark's mind. A one-word cataclysm, a three-syllable verdict offered by a doctor posing as a judge but in a white smock instead of a black robe.

"She has her good days, and her bad days."

They drove in silence for a while, a twitchy Boyle gazing out the window and scanning the terrain for suspects. Stark plucked the Death Donut off the dashboard and gobbled it down.

His thoughts drifted as he reached into the bag for a second donut, recalling his own rookie year some three decades past when, like Boyle, he was filled with idealistic enthusiasm. Most cops, he reflected, had seen it all.

He was the cop who hadn't.

Stark had been on the force for thirty years. No one had ever shot at him and he had shot at no one.

He had never helped break up a riot. He had never rescued a hostage. He had never saved anyone from a burning building. He had never talked down a potential suicide from a building ledge.

He had never been The Hero.

Once, though — the irony was almost, but not quite, comical — he had been summoned to the scene of a breaking-and-entering. A mere boy, he had been told, was up to no good. The boy he busted was his own son and only child, Kevin, then fourteen years old. Stark had even pointed his gun at the boy until he realized who it was. Kevin had gone on to become a career criminal and was now serving ten to twenty for armed robbery, downstate at the penitentiary they called Big Muddy.

Stark sighed anew.

He regarded himself as a failure, and his functional life was almost done. Once he had consoled himself with an old tract that had first surfaced back around the 1920s about Springfield's most famous local boy: "Lincoln's Failures."

Failed in business   — *1831*
Defeated for Legislature — *1832*
Sweetheart died   — *1835*
Nervous breakdown   — *1836*

And so on. "A Failure at 50," the tract had proclaimed, "and elected president at 51." But now Stark was Lincoln's age one year before Lincoln died, and success seemed as distant as ever.

"Sarge," Boyle said. "Check it out."

Stark's eyes drifted apathetically in the direction of Boyle's curt nod.

Both cops fixed their attention on the stovepipe hat.

"I think it's a suspect," Boyle said.

"They're called African-Americans, now, son, not 'suspects,'" Stark said in a mildly reproving tone of voice, thinking about the sensitivity training courses that all Springfield cops were required periodically to take, sandwiched between the new courses on the use of military surplus equipment like body armor, mine-resistant trucks, automatic rifles with silencers, even tanks: part of the never-ending War on Terror. (War on Terra?) In his short time on the force, Boyle had already often expressed the desire to patrol Springfield in a Humvee or from the turret of a tank and "blow the Bad Guys to Kingdom Come."

"Besides," Stark added, "I don't think he's black. It's a trick of light and shadow, and the black clothes he's wearing."

"You sure? He looks tall enough to play in the NBA."

Stark stopped the car.

The cops clambered out of it and approached the man, whose stovepipe hat made him nearly seven feet tall. The sun was above and behind him so he looked more like a silhouette than a man, but gradually the cops' eyes adjusted and they could see the details of his time-bitten face. His cheeks were violently sunken and his cheekbones jutted out. One of them showed through the flesh, like an elbow through a hole in a shirt. He was staring with incredulity at the squad car that had just rolled to a stop. "How's it possible?" he asked, in a keening, unpleasant voice that sounded like fingernails raking across a blackboard. "By jings, what galvanizes this thing? Boys, *where's the horse?*"

"The horse?" both cops inquired as one in mystification.

The tall man swept a long, lanky arm at the intermittent traffic. "What are they, boys? Carriages without horses? What makes 'em go?"

"A Lincoln impersonator," Boyle announced, not too surprised. Springfield was full of them. This guy, though, looked *exactly* like the guy on the five dollar bill, Boyle thought, but also like a homeless bum just off a bender. The great man was filthy. He reeked of rot, and Boyle wrinkled his nose in an effort to stanch the stench. Stark was suspicious. Along with rot, he smelled a rat. He was about to ask the man for his ID when both he and Boyle noticed the hole in the man's cheek where the bone showed through.

But the skin was regrowing as they watched. Two cop mouths fell open.

Boyle snatched his gun from his holster and went into a defensive crouch. Hands shaking, he pointed the gun at the animate scarecrow. "Hands up!" he yelled. "Hands up!"

Lincoln regarded Boyle with bewilderment.

"What's under that hat, mister?" Boyle demanded.

"Beg pardon, young man?"

"A dirty nuclear bomb? You got a dirty bomb under that hat, fella?"

The scarecrow offered a lopsided, uncomprehending grin.

"Move your hands slowly, very slowly, toward your head, and then, mister, *remove that hat.*"

Stark leaned down toward his crouching partner, laid a hand on his shoulder and said, "Rob, I don't think —"

"I know what I'm doing, Sarge!"

Lincoln removed his hat. When he did, the sparrow flew off.

"Well," he drawled, "there goes my soul, I reckon. Or maybe it's just my land-grant program."

Boyle jerked the gun upward, took aim and shot the bird out of the sky. It exploded in a cloud of feathers, and its corpse fell into the tall grass just off the road shoulder.

With a practiced gesture Stark relieved Boyle of his gun and then emptied it of its bullets before handing it back to him. He had learned this trick from watching reruns of the Andy Griffith show.

The tall man batted a hand at the buzzing flies that were circulating about his head, temporarily dispersing them, and then touched with his nail-clawed fingertips his cheek, the regrowing flesh. "Well," he drawled, in the studied way of an accomplished cracker-barrel raconteur, "one time I wrote a state paper in which I used the phrase, 'Broken eggs caint be mended.' Now my advisers, including Mr. Seward, they persuaded me not to use that phrase, judgin' it 'undignified.' But now by the look o' things, boys, I reckon maybe broken eggs *can* be mended." The hole in the cheek closed up.

Sergeant Stark recovered his aplomb and said, "Sir, may we see some ID, please?"

"Eye Dee?"

"Identification."

"Why, young man, I'm Abraham Lincoln."

"A Lincoln impersonator, yes, sir, we understand," Stark said. "But we need to know your *real* name. Who you really are. Do you have a driver's license?" Boyle was silent, still in a defensive crouch and pointing the emptied gun at the interloper.

"A what?"

"A state ID? A Social Security card? Can you prove who you are?"

Abraham Lincoln looked bemused, gray eyes dancing with latent mischief. He leaned down toward the men over whom he towered and said with a captivating grin, "I'm Abe Lincoln, boys. What year is this? I'm afraid I've been asleep for a long, lazy time. Normally I'm used to sleeping like the old woman's dance: short and sweet. By the look o' things, I reckon I've overslept this time."

The cops were silent.

"I'm Abe Lincoln," Lincoln repeated with homey conviction, stretching out a hand clawed with nine-inch nails. "What are you boys named?"

Bewildered, Stark timidly touched Lincoln's hand, avoiding the nails, and introduced himself and his partner, who had backed away like a cornered animal, shaking all over and still pointing the emptied gun at the tall man. Then Sergeant Stark said, "You'd best come with us, sir."

Lincoln fixed Boyle with a long, lazy, lingering stare, his face somehow simian. He did not smile, and he did not frown.

His expression was inscrutable.

$$\frac{\overline{||}}{\underset{\overline{V}}{(oo)}}$$

He was born Wally Wiener, a name as humiliating to him as if he had been born a boy named Sue.

When he reached adulthood, which, for him, was adolescence by other means, he legally changed his name to Jefferson Davis Shitkicker Freedom, known to The Gang as "Shit Free or Die," or sometimes just "Shit Free," or sometimes even just "Shit." (That would be that Commie bastard Red Dave talking, fuck his pink eyes.)

Today he was driving his pickup truck in the mountains of Idaho: snowcaps blindingly white under the sun in a cloudless blue sky. Steep canyons, frothing rapids. An eagle swooped and dived, its shadow gliding serenely over the land. God's country. It was ten in the morning on April 15, 2015.

Shit Free had the windows of his pickup rolled down and the free air of Idaho was whipping through his hair, which was tied back in a ponytail. His guns were in the rack in the pickup's rear. From the antenna a frayed Confederate battle flag, the Southern Cross, snapped in the wind. Ted Nugent was wailing on the radio. Shit Free's guitar was in the backseat. On the passenger's side seat next to him was a six-pack of locally brewed Gutbuster beer, of which it was said that it would make a real man outta ya by eating a hole in your gut because it contained sulfuric acid. If you could survive that, you could survive anything. What don't kill ya, makes ya stronger. The six-pack sat atop the morning edition of the Idaho Statesman. A banner headline in bright Red State red ink blazed across the top of the paper: IDAHO VOTES SECESH!

Shit Free stamped on the gas pedal and pushed the speedometer needle toward eighty. "Yee-haw!" he yelled, catching sight of his reflection in the truck's side mirror: the wide-brimmed cowboy hat, the wraparound shades, the coiled snake tattoo on a muscular shoulder showing from underneath the black vest he wore, no shirt underneath. Grappling the wheel with expert but nerve-jangling verve, with devil-may-care derring-do, he effortlessly negotiated a couple of hairpin turns at such speed that at one point he was driving on only two wheels, the pickup listing at a perilous forty-five-degree angle and laying rubber on the road. When the road straightened he gentled the truck back down to four wheels and slackened his speed.

He pulled over to the road shoulder, parked the truck and turned up the radio. Rockabilly. He reached for a bottle of Gutbuster. He considered for a moment the twist-off cap. Then a lazy, contemptuous but somehow seductive grin sprawled across his face, like a hooker stretching out on a cheap hotel-room bed. Holding the bottle, he snatched up the copy of the Statesman and got out of the pickup. He found a boulder and smashed the neck of the bottle on it, causing the bottle top to explode in splinters and the foamy beer to ejaculate. He considered the shards of the neck of the decapitated bottle, and then put those daggers inside his mouth and took a guzzle of Gutbuster, half draining the bottle. He cut his lips and tongue. He spat beer and blood and bits of glass, belched, and then set the bottle down on the boulder and patted his beer belly, in which the beer sloshed and, he hoped, was beginning to eat a hole into his stomach lining. He then held the Statesman stretched out between his fingers and again read the headline. There was an ad on Page One, paid for, the fine print said, by someone named Homer (Homo?) Hickenlooper: NOBAMA, an industrial-strength font shouted, below a crude, chimp-like caricature of the president circumscribed by a thick red circle with a diagonal red slash across the president's face. He read the first paragraph under the fiery red main headline:

"Joining fourteen other southern and Rocky Mountain states, the Idaho State Legislature today voted to secede from the United Socialist States of America."

Shit Free read slowly, moving his lips as he did. As he mentally tiptoed his way to the end of the seemingly interminable twenty-three-word sentence, another grin ripped open his face. His two upper front teeth were missing, but his lower teeth were intact and had skulls and crossbones tattooed into them. Below the fold was an item about Idaho's unsolved rural murders, ten of them so far.

Movement caught his attention in a gully far below, next to a babbling brook lined with glittering stones: probably precious Idaho gems, the kind of stuff that would make Idaho self-reliant except for the tyranny of Washington. Some hiker, some faggot with a cane, was making his way along the bank of the flashing stream. Shit Free returned to his pickup and fetched a pair of binoculars.

He tracked the man. He noted, with anger, that the man was dressed funny. Wearing knickers like a fag. He looked up and down the highway. Not a car in sight. He fetched a 30-ought-six from the rack of the pickup, trained the gun sights on the man and pulled the trigger. The rifle banged and bucked, pitching him backward. Smoke curled. When he looked down at the gully again, he saw that the faggot was lying facedown upon the rocks, a pool of blood seeping out of his shattered skull. Shit Free made a mental note to have another skull tattooed in another tooth. They were like notches in a belt, for him. There had been ten unsolved rural murders so far, and ten tattooed teeth.

Make that eleven on both counts.

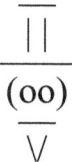

"When and where would you like to live?"

It was a plush, postmodernist office in Seattle, a tinted plate-glass window offering a sweeping view of downtown dominated by the Space Needle. The sky was unexpectedly clear, the notorious Seattle rain having abated after an overnight downpour that had left the city squeaky clean, the sunlight glittering and dancing off of every window and polished surface. The thick traffic moved on the streets below and from this height the vehicles resembled marching ants on the prowl for prey.

Alexander World sat behind a desk metaphorically as big as a continent. The name of his firm, DREAM-WORLDS, showed backward into the office on part of the fronting window, the letters arranged to face the city and not the office. They cast elongated, abstract shadows on the carpet. The office held a hodgepodge of furniture of varied historical style, all mixed together in a repudiation of architectural and decorative meta-narratives.

"There is no truth," Alexander World suddenly announced to his client, who had appeared before him like a supplicant before a priest. "There is only want, and need, and usually greed."

Alexander World was the entrepreneur who had burst unexpectedly upon the stage of history in early 2014 and had been dubbed "Alexander the Great" by Time Magazine, which had named him Person and/or Machine of the Year. A blown-up version of the cover of that issue graced one wall of his office, framed in plain, unpretentious wood, not gilt as some might have anticipated.

World was fond of speaking in cryptic and sometimes apocalyptic aphorisms, fancying himself the Frederich Nietzsche of the Digital Age. The company that he had founded had engineered a breakthrough in quantum computing that had made possible computational wonders beyond previous conceivability. The breakthrough involved isolating polarized light in such a way that the previously incompatible conjugate paired properties of the wavelike photons, such as momentum and location, could simultaneously be measured to arbitrary accuracy, thus overthrowing Heisenberg's Uncertainty Principle. World's revolution was as great as the Uncertainty Principle revolution it was overthrowing. Revolution is ever in the air. The King is dead, long live the King.

"God is dead, love live God," Alexander the Great added, slamming a fist on his desk. His supplicant flinched. He was awed (or affected to be awed) to be in the presence of this brazen buccaneer, just thirty years young. Conqueror of the known Cyber World. "That means you are God, sir. You must make your own reality."

World, wearing an ordinary white dress shirt and a pair of blue jeans, sat with his bare, gym-toned muscular arms crossed over his chest, his sleeves rolled up in workmanlike, let's-get-down-to-brass-tacks fashion. The supplicant was an elderly, seemingly shy man who held in front of him a sixties-style fedora with a felt band around the base. His dress was nothing special: a corduroy suit coat evidently bought off the rack at the Goodwill store, baggy gray old man's pants. Open-necked shirt collar, no tie. Ketchup stain above the shirt pocket. It looked like dried blood. The man's flaccid facial flesh resembled melted candle wax on the wick of his scrawny neck, and he had the startled eyes of a deer in headlights behind wire-rimmed glasses that slanted down on his crooked nose. A few stray wisps of white hair curled up from his otherwise cue-ball head like question marks. When frightened, as he often was (or affected to be) those question marks boinged upward into exclamation points. He was named Homer Hickenlooper, and he was a wealthy recluse who was reputed to be daft. He had never married and had no heirs, and he was eighty years old. Some bloggers styled him the Howard Hughes of the 21st century, though they were usually drunk when they did so.

Before granting this appointment, which Hickenlooper had requested in a rather obsequious formal letter, World had reviewed what he knew about the man. He was a real estate magnate. His speciality was luxury high-rise condos for the nouveau-riche, done in an architectural style that one critic had famously derided as "a toxic marriage of bombast and kitsch, the architectural equivalent of cheap bowling trophies inflated to grotesque size." The magnate was also vaguely connected to shadowy conspiracy theory networks, which he purportedly financed, at least in part: The 9/11 Truther movement and the Obama Birther crazies, for instance. He lived with a retinue of servants in a Gatsbyesque mansion near San Francisco. For some reason, he had caused to be planted on its grounds a sprawling labyrinth made of hedges, perhaps because over the years Hickenlooper's name had been linked to labyrinthine shady dealings and crimes including murder, but nothing had been proved. He had been indicted three times, but all three indictments had been quashed under questionable circumstances. The man was a mystery, more maze than man, more persona than person. His Web site had no site map and was password-protected. But no one knew the password.

World thought that this man seemed like the photographic negative of another famous real-estate magnate, popularly know as The Donald, a bombastic con artist who was making noises about running for president. Here was Hickenlooper the cagey hermit with virtually no hair, versus The Donald, the narcissistic showman with a full head of orange hair. World now wondered:

Who was more dangerous?

Having just been informed that he was God, Hickenlooper demurred, unlike The Donald would have. He set his hat on the desk and searched for something Godlike to say. World leaned toward him, clasped his hands on the desktop and said: "You realize, sir, that Dreamworlds technology is expensive. *Very* expensive."

"I can afford it," Hickenlooper vowed in a keening, nasal voice that World found sickening. After a pause, the magnate asked: "Son, may I inquire as to your business model? If only a few rich people can afford what you make — "

World cut him off. Hickenlooper was a real estate man. But World knew that the old man knew nothing about *virtual* real estate, also known as virtstate, which was World's stock in trade.

World opened a drawer, took out a pair of wraparound glasses, black lenses and yellow frames, and tossed them at the old man, who, startled, caught them. "Put them on," World invited.

The man looked questioningly at the glasses. Looking up at World, the latter nodded reassuringly and repeated, "Put them on."

"Why?"

"If you put on those glasses, you'll enter an entirely different world."

The man grudgingly put them on.

He gasped.

He was indeed in a completely different world, a 3D, immersive new reality. The landscape was rocky and barren. A warlock with wings and the face of a gargoyle flew toward him, holding a spear, against the backdrop of a towering castle perched on a precipice and silhouetted against a sky boiling with flames, lava and ash. The warlock raced toward the magnate on majestically flapping wings and then reared back and hurled the spear. It sped toward the center of Hickenlooper's head, the target between his eyes. The old man ripped the wrap from his face and flung it down on the desktop just before the spear struck him. The question-mark hairs atop his head had boinged upward into exclamation points of terror.

"My heart," he gasped, clapping a weathered hand over his chest. His heart was pounding, pounding. One could almost see it pounding, like a cartoon heart, making his covering hand go up and down.

In a voice tremulous with terror, Hickenlooper demanded of World: "What would have happened if — if I had not removed the glasses, just in time? Before that spear struck?" Offering the old man a thin grin, World maintained a cagey silence. He liked to keep the clients guessing.

"The shades are called DreamGlass, Mr. Hickenlooper," World said, ending the smiling silence. "Mass produced at an affordable price. That's how we make our money: Games. Virtual reality, the next step. Immersive, real. As real as the real world. Qubits. Quantum bits. But they're still just games, and they are the same for everyone. This is what the young do today, to escape. They escape into our glasses, in which they can also surf the Web, text their friends, download video, view porn and so on. A rising generation of Vbots, blundering mindlessly about on the streets, mesmerized by the visions in their wraparounds while they collide with pedestrians because they can't see what is real but only what is virtually real or surreal. These kids don't socialize with their peers. They socialize with Warlocks, Warlords, Wizards, Space Aliens, Gods and Demons. They don't go outside anymore. They go inside." World tapped the side of his head with an index finger. "Into inner space. I'm sure you'll agree that these shades put Google Glass in the shade. But the wearers of DreamGlass see through a glass darkly. They're just too young and dumb to know it. However, we give the public what it wants."

"Escape," the man muttered hopefully, and World was disgusted to see strands of milky saliva tethering Hickenlooper's upper lip to his lower. Despite his wealth, his teeth were bad, little crooked tombstones in the bloody soil of his gums. He suddenly hated Hickenlooper, and almost wished that the magnate's experience with the warlock in virtstate had given him a heart attack. But the man's racing heart had slowed to a canter and would likely serve him another ten years, maybe twenty with a stent, like Dick Cheney. Only the good (and poor) die young,

World thought moodily.

"But for the few who are wealthy, Mr. Hickenlooper, we do custom-made worlds that are as real as they so-called real world."

"What do you mean, the 'so-called real world,' Mr. World?"

"How do you know you're not already living in a simulation, Mr. Hickenlooper? Maybe you have been your whole life, and have never known it."

"You mean like that movie, The Matrix?"

"Yeah. Or like a brain in a vat. Or like Descartes' evil demon. The idea goes back a long time, actually. What is the world, anyway, but a simulation of the mind? And what are we but avatars in our own personal video games? *Esse est percipi*, Mr. Hickenlooper. 'To be is to be perceived.' Bishop Berkeley said that centuries ago."

"I'm afraid you're losing me, Mr. World."

"Do you know what the quantum measurement problem is, Mr. Hickenlooper?"

"No."

"There is no reality until a measurement is made. Prior to a measurement by a human mind, the detector needles are set to every possible position. What does that tell you about so-called reality?"

"I don't know. All I want to do is live back in my youth."

"When and where?"

"The early sixties."

"Explain."

"The early nineteen sixties," the man repeated apologetically, his rheumy eyes misting over with the milky glaucoma of nostalgia. "I was in my mid-twenties, then, just starting out. The world was a better place. It was my oyster."

"A better place, Mr. Hickenlooper? How so? I seem to recall that in 1962, there nearly was a nuclear war over Cuba."

"An innocent time, Mr. World. Before all the ... you know, before the *changes*." Those euphemistic changes. World bristled at this racist bastard.

Bridling his anger, he raised his arms, bent them at the elbows and intertwined his fingers behind his head while he leaned back in his leather swivel chair and regarded the meek old man (or was he feigning meekness?) who sat supplicatory before him, begging to be freed from the world of 2015 that was coming apart at the seams. Silence. Then Hickenlooper mustered his courage and became dogmatic, rattling off the horrors of today, one by one, counting them off by repeatedly pressing down one index finger with the other: "Climate change ... the ice caps melting, the tides rising. Debt out of control. Socialism in Washington. Muslim terrorists — just like this new gang, The Paradise 72 Brigades Inc., which has conducted a hostile takeover of huge swathes of the Middle East. Now *they've* got a business plan, Mr. World! I've studied it. I may even *invest* in it. Then there's the breakup of the United States. Yesterday, another state voted to secede. Idaho. There's going to be a new Confederacy, or a second Civil War, or both. Red States vs. Blue States. The world is having a nervous breakdown."

"Blacks knew their place," World retorted angrily, speaking of the early nineteen-sixties. "A black president was unthinkable. Women busied themselves in the kitchen or in the secretarial pool. Queers were in the closet. There was no Internet, no social media, no way for people of similar interests to connect with one another except by luck or circumstance. The Cold War. A nuclear sword of Damocles. The Vietnam War on the horizon. JFK slain, then later King and RFK. The past always looks better in the rear-view mirror, Mr. Hickenlooper. Nostalgia," he intoned, pretentiously speaking aphoristically, "is the last refugee of the temporal refugee without a mimetic memory — without a Time to call Now, like a man with no place to call home."

"Mr. World, do you know what the Dark Enlightenment is?"

"No."

The hairs atop Hickenlooper's head slowly curled upward from question marks to exclamation points, like snakes charmed out of baskets by dark flute music.

He leaned forward and offered a slimy smile, and patted World on the hand. "Now it's my turn to ask questions you can't answer, young man. Funnily, you present yourself as a self-reliant, world-conquering buccaneer, but from our conversation today I take it you are a conventional, run-of-the-mill, bleeding-heart liberal. A dime a dozen. Yet no one was more made for the Dark Enlightenment than you. Son, you truly could rule the world — not just the cyberworld, but the *actual* world. You have what it takes." Hickenlooper winked sinisterly.

World drew himself up sharply and stiffened in his seat.

"My understanding, Mr. World, is that you can build me an immersive virtual world of the early 1960s, but not only that. Understand, Mr. World, that I don't want to be in that world and know it's make-believe. I want to be in that world and believe it is the only real world. I want to forget all about this world, as if it never existed at all. You can do that? Is that my understanding?"

"Yes. But that will cost you a mega-fortune, sir."

"And that's not all."

"What else?"

"I don't want that history to go the way it did, as the decade went on. I want it to go the way I want it to go."

"Like how?"

"I want Goldwater elected, for example."

"A mega, mega, mega-fortune."

"And I want to be young again, to feel myself back in my youth."

"The pot of gold at the end of the rainbow."

"How much, Mr. World?"

A few minutes later, after practically bum-rushing the malignant magnate out of his office, Alexander World sat behind his desk and stared with incredulity at the check that Hickenlooper had casually tossed off with an indifferent flourish of his gold-plated pen. He held it stretched out between his fingers. As he contemplated the sum, the sun vanished behind a cloud. It was as if a shadow were passing over him personally, and only him.

Marking him.

He laid the cheek on the desktop, rose to his feet and gazed out the window. The depressing Seattle rain was back. A previously clear sky was now gray. Shaky rivulets of rain wandered down the plate-glass window like tears, and the Space Needle and the rest of downtown Seattle became a watercolor in which the paints were running. His cellphone's ringtone was "Dark Side of the Moon" by Pink Floyd. He learned from his phone that he was shorter of breath and one day closer to death.

"Babe."

"Cassie."

"I'm pregnant."

World goggled at the phone.

"Just got the news ... Alex? You there?"

"Sure, I'm here. Just trying to absorb the shock of the ... good news."

"Well, you don't sound too happy about it."

"It's something else ... well, more good news. It's just a shock, that's all. Your good news, and my good news."

"What? What's your good news?"

World stared at the check.

"Alex?"

"Cassie, I'm desperately happy for you, for us, I'm just overwhelmed, of course. Unfortunately I've got an urgent meeting *right now*. I'll call you later. Love you to pieces."

"Babe?"

He cut her off.

The rain ticked on the windowpane.

He sat down, laid the check aside and booted his laptop.

He surfed to cnn.com, and the usual blazing headlines about the breakup of America. He was too distracted to process the breaking news about the breakup, and the secesh rally in Washington going on right now. Instead his eyes wandered down to the little headlines, the links farther down the page underlined in blue and written in the folksy, childish, imbecilic cyberlingo that passed for online (and even print) journalese these days: OMG! Watch vid of Beyonce twerking! ... Amazeballs! Dog pushes cat into blender and turns it on! Must-see vid! ... Paradise 72 Brigades: WTF? Threat or menace? Join the online discussion with Newt Gingrich ... Phew! What's up with Hillary's new Lesbo 'do? ... Donald Trump weighs presidential run under the slogan, 'We shall overcomb.'

Mortified by this moronic rubbish, he looked again at the masthead, thinking he might have surfed to The Onion by mistake. But no, it was cnn.com. He refreshed the page.

BREAKING NEWS: LINCOLN TOMB ROBBED.

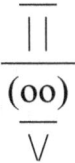

"I am Cy Clone. The whirlwind of the world. Good mourning, America!"

"Good mourning, Cy!" A hundred thousand full-throated voices roared in animal unison, defenders of individualism and liberty roaring as one. Liberty's lockstep. A great many of these rugged individualists were identically dressed in the pantaloons, powdered wigs and frilly collars of the Revolutionary War era. They had assembled on the Mall in the nation's capital with fake flintlock rifles and barrels of tea. Giant video screens erected at the foot of the Lincoln Memorial were showing Cyrus (Cy) Clone's Webcast from a secret location: an underground bunker somewhere in the wastelands of the Old Confederacy, that phoenix rising from the ashes of a Civil War that never actually ended but, like a dormant virus atavistic, was again eating away at the body politic. The Battle of the Blue and Gray had just shifted hue, to become the Battle of the Blue States and the Red States.

"Do you remember," Cyclone yelled, "Ronald Reagan's 'Morning in America?'"

Reagan. The name was magic. The crowd went nuts at the mere utterance of it, even though Reagan had raised their taxes eleven times and had never proposed a balanced budget.

"Well, now we've got Mourning in America. Not morning. Mourning. M-O-U-R-N-I-N-G." The mob around the Mall roared. A few women, fanning themselves with newspapers, swooned. Many others swayed, fingers splayed, arms stretched out, eyes closed and faces agog with ecstasy and slathered in sweat, as if Cyclone were talking in tongues at a tent revivalist meeting and they were swept up in the drama of it all, the epiphany, the Rapture.

The giant screens showed a middle-aged man with a round moon face. Ill-fitting suit and tie. Perspiring. Pink cheeks, thinning gray hair on top. Eyes polar. Mouth a downturned boomerang of pure ignorant hate and rage. He sat before a bare steel desk, peering into the Webcam. He drummed his fingers on the desktop. He was flanked on the left by a Don't Tread on Me yellow snake flag and on the right by a stack of shotguns propped up against the wall like cords of firewood. Nothing else. The room gave the impression of an austere prison cell, or of what it supposedly was: a spartan underground bunker fortified with flags, guns, guts, grit, canned foods, provisions, privations and patriotism against the collapse to come, the collapse of civilization. It was said that the bunker was stocked with End of the World biscuits and the Time of Trouble tub, which contained 7,728 servings of black-bean burger pouches. These provisions had been purchased at marked-up prices from Jim and Tammy Bakker's online Apocalypse Specialty Store.

Cyclone leaned toward the Webcam, waved his fists and yelled, his cheeks growing sunset red:

"The tree of liberty must be refreshed from time to time with the blood of patriots and tyrants! It is its natural manure!"

Roars. Jefferson's quote about the Tree of Liberty, blood and manure never failed to impress. It was rhetorical cocaine.

The portly, red-faced man leapt to his feet. He

paced in circles and gesticulated. He huffed and puffed, he ranted and raved. He spoke, actually, in tongues. He did not speak in complete sentences but in buzzwords: Obamacare. Death panels. Benghazi. Bergdahl. Al Qaeda. Big Government. Socialism. Muslims and atheists, who apparently were identical. Freedom. Morality. God. At last a ham fist smashed down on the steel desk to punctuate the final buzzword: Secession! Bang!

The lights and cameras went off. Cyclone was not actually in a bunker in the wastelands of the Old Confederacy. He was in a studio in Burbank, California. His exhortations had exhausted him, and as the camera crew struck the props he reclined in his chair, unknotted his tie and drew a handkerchief from the breast pocket of his suit coat. He dabbed the hanky at the constellation of sweat dots on his forehead and then with it he wiped the makeup from his face, the rouge that had rage-reddened his cheeks, but it was faux fury for a fairy. His racing heart slowed to an amble, and he exhaled. He said: "It's hard work gulling the rubes, but it's a living. And if it speeds up the crackup of the U.S., all the better. Let those damned slaveholder-wannabes have their New Confederacy at last, and see how long they last. In a few years they'll be begging to reunite and coming hat in hand to Washington for bailouts."

His husband, John, moved behind him and began massaging his shoulders. "There, there," John said. He leaned downward and kissed the whirlwind of the world on the cheek. "Calm down, darling. Think of your blood pressure."

CHAPTER 2
WHAT IN TARNATION?

At the Springfield precinct police station house, Abraham Lincoln asked to "warsh up in a warshbasin." Officer Sully Stark showed him to a bathroom. Lincoln marveled at the clean toilets and sinks. The gleaming porcelain, the tiled floor. Soap from a hand dispenser!

Afterward he leaned back in a swivel chair on the other side of a desk from Officers Boyle and Stark. A "cheer," Lincoln pronounced the word "chair." The clean bathroom had got him in the mood for a story, and he regaled the pop-eyed officers with his famous tale of Ethan Allen, the outhouse, the "pitcher," as he put it, of George "Warshington" on the outhouse wall, and instantaneous shitting. When he proffered the punchline, Officer Sully Stark guffawed. He had never heard the story before, obviously having missed Steven Spielberg's "Lincoln." The idealistic officer Boyle, by contrast, looked mortified. When Stark's laughter died down, he became glum and suspicious again. He was about to retire, and the last thing that he needed, at the end of a long career wasted on banalities, was this lank-boned, sad-faced mystery sprawled ungainly in his "cheer" before him. Who was this man, really, and what to do with him? He couldn't rightly be arrested for he hadn't done anything wrong so far as Stark knew. Then the president told an old "nigger" joke from his half-remembered youth, speaking in Negro dialect, which further mortified and also saddened Officer

Boyle, who thought of black people not as niggers but as suspects, but the joke made Officer Stark snort with laughter. The president saw a laptop computer on the desk, the lid raised but the screen blank, and asked in lazy drawl, "What is that thing, boys?"

"It's a laptop," Officer Boyle said, puzzled by the question.

"A laptop," the president drawled in a dreamy, reminiscent way. Inspired, he told a ribald yarn about some whore whom he had once had on the prairie who did what today would be called a lap dance before the two of them got down to bidness. "Way back then the boys called me 'The Prairie Dawg,'" Lincoln offered with a wink. Officer Boyle again looked mortified. He even blushed. But Officer Stark grinned knowingly and lasciviously. He was warming up to this man. Sully Stark dearly loved his wife Hortense, but he had been young once, too.

Lincoln sighed, looked off gray-eyed into middle distance and said, "I was always afraid that the reason Molly was crazy as a loon was because I'd given her the French pox. It's a guilt that ain't left me in a coon's age."

"French pox?" Stark asked.

"Syphilis, son."

Officer Boyle lectured Lincoln: "Lincoln impersonators, sir, are supposed to recite the Gettysburg Address and be a role model. Not tell stories about ... uh, defecation, and, uh, ladies of the night. Or, uh, STDs. Also, you're supposed to use a deep voice. Like Gregory Peck when he played you in a movie. And not talk in slang."

The president squinted in vague remembrance, and then it came to him. "Oh, that little thing," he said with a lopsided grin. "My remarks at Gettysburg. I reckon that speech didn't scour. I prefer my Second Inaugural Address." He pronounced "Inaugural" as "Innagerel" in his oddly squeaky voice. "The Gettysburg Address was a flat failure."

Officer Boyle said: "The Gettysburg Address is one of the most famous speeches of all time, sir. I memorized it as a schoolboy."

Lincoln looked contemplatively at Officer Boyle. The hairs stood up on the back of the cop's neck. He suddenly felt like a hen without a house in the vicinity of a fox without scruples.

"You boys got any vittles?" Lincoln asked after a long, uneasy silence.

"Vittles?"

"Man works up a powerful hunger while asleep."

The cops traded glances. "Food," they guessed.

Officer Boyle had been seriously contemplating the possibility that this was Zombie Lincoln. The idea appealed to his sense of gun justice: A quick shot to the head, and this enigmatic episode would be over.

"Would you like some brains?" Boyle blurted out.

Lincoln looked abstractedly at Boyle.

"An apple'll do me," the president drawled after a pause. "Apples agree with me. And a cup of Adam's Ale."

"Adam's ale?" Stark asked.

"Water, boys. It's the strongest thing I drink." Officer Stark, who from time to time enjoyed Gutbuster beer imported form Idaho, was disappointed by this intelligence, but Officer Boyle, a teetotaler, nodded approvingly, though he was saddened by the failure of his brains gambit.

"I cain't take my vittles regular, so I kinder just browse 'round," the president sighed.

They fetched him an apple and a glass of water. They watched as he bit into the apple with a loud crunch. He drank the water in one swig and devoured the apple in four big bites. He then pitched the core into a nearby wastebasket with an easy, lank motion of his long, black-clad arm, like a softball pitcher tossing underhand.

Then Lincoln studied his clawed fingernails. He pulled out a pocket knife and started cutting them off, with the easy, practiced gestures of a man whittling wood. The cops watched with rapt incredulity. Lincoln called the knife his "Arkansas toothpick." As he trimmed his nails, he looked again at the laptop and drawled, "What does that thing do, anyhow, boys? Why does it have all them little squares with letters and numbers on 'em?" Lincoln had never even seen a typewriter.

Officer Boyle booted the computer.

Lincoln straightened in his "cheer," laid aside his Arkansas toothpick and watched the movements on the screen. He had never seen a computer. He had never seen a TV. He had never even seen a movie. He scrutinized the device intently, with fierce intelligence and catlike curiosity. The country bumpkin imposture was over. An unnerved Officer Boyle thought: this dude is as serious as a heart attack. He may be dangerous.

"What in tarnation?" Lincoln gasped, as the icons at the bottom of the screen and the photo of a galaxy sprawled across it came into view. "Is it a magic trick? Boys, explain it to me, please."

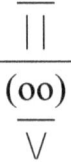

Shit Free rolled his pickup to a stop in the parking lot of the Drink Here Bar in the little hole of a town called Whitely, Idaho. It had swinging Old West saloon doors and when he banged through them all the regulars were present, drinking early and often. The Gang. His girlfriend was among 'em. Her name was Becky. He called her The Bike, as in, Ride the Bike. She was already drunk. She wore blue-denim cutoff short shorts. She knocked Shit out with her American thighs. Platform shoes. A clinging T-shirt, braless, bodacious tits jiggling as she danced drunkenly by herself to that goddamned hip-hop shit on the Internet jukebox.

I love bad bitches, that's my fuckin problem
And yeah I like to fuck, I got a fuckin problem
I love bad bitches, that's my fuckin problem
And yeah I like to fuck I got a fuckin problem

Shit Free pulled out a pistol and shot the jukebox. It exploded in a neon nova. Shards of metal, glass and plastic whizzed through the air like shrapnel. The Gang reeled from this blast. Pieces of the playlist clattered down on the bar counter. The bartender was preposterously old. His name was Sam. He had been tending bar at Drink Here since arriving by foot out of nowhere, out of the dust, alone and with a battered suitcase, in Whitely, Idaho, in 1989, more than a quarter-century ago. He was mostly silent about his past, except for a few choice but enigmatic stories involving risqué foreign escapades, but as a bartender he was nonpareil. He commanded respect because of his age — people called him the Ancient of Days — and because he seemed to be an intellectual. Normally intellectuals would be as welcome in Whitely as locusts or fags, but Sam was different. He had a way of articulating meaninglessness, of giving voice to the void. The locals sensed that something about the world, *their* world, was amiss: not just trivially so or in the particulars of their own drab lives, but *cosmically* amiss, cataclysmically *off*. Yet because they lacked the education or aptitude to articulate their amorphous discontent, they remained perpetually frustrated and fell back on guns and God to impart meaning to their world. Or so President Obama had once condescendingly said in his usual elitist way. Sam, though, unlike the snobbish president, had a way of understanding and verbalizing what the locals only dimly felt. In addition to the Ancient of Days, people called him the Big Ear, for the patient and sympathetic way in which he listened to the sob stories of Drink Here Bar's regulars, those tattooed miscreants, malcontents, poets, dreamers, Socialists, Libertarians, Anarchists, Objectivists, survivalists and alcoholics (or all of the above) who formed the core of the Gang to which Shit Free or Die belonged. Sam was Irish. Today he wore his usual white smock, his sleeves rolled up as he cleaned a mug with a wet rag and peered down at a fragment of the playbill from the assassinated Internet jukebox on the bar counter, advertising the song that the machine had been playing when Shit shot it.

He asked Shit Free: "Why'd you do that, son? Why'd you kill A$AP Rocky?"

"*Je ne sais pas, Monsieur*," someone piped up, and the room exploded in laughter at the inside joke based on a tale that Sam had once told about himself. It relieved the tension.

Clopping on her platform shoes, her American thighs patriotically jiggling, Becky the Bike flew into hysterics. She attacked Shit Free. She pounded on his chest with her fists, but he seized her wrists and flung her to the floor on her ass. She sprang saucily to her feet on those beautiful legs in the cutoffs and platforms and again attacked Shit Free. She was babbling hysterically, a monologue spiced with obscenities. Shit Free got her in a headlock, and had to hold on tight because holding on to her when she got pissed was a little like trying to hold on to a tiger or maybe a cyclone. Or a bike without brakes. As she flailed and fought he tightened his muscular, tattooed arms around her neck and called her a goddamned whore. "I don't want to come into my hangout and hear that goddamn nigger music," he roared at her. "You know that, you goddamned whore!" She kneed him in the balls in his tight jeans and he let go of her. His hands angled down to his crotch and she raked her fingernails across his cheek, drawing blood. He raised his hands and she aimed a kick at his crotch. When the toe of her platform shoe arced up to bust his balls he caught her by the ankle, which had a panther tattoo on it. He yanked her upward and threw her back down on the floor on her ass again. A competing hubbub of voices sprang up, and then the other members of the gang intervened to keep the lovers separated. Sam kept cleaning beer mugs with his damp rag, watching the scene unfold with the detached demeanor of someone who had seen too much in life to be impressed by this silly set-to.

Becky the Bike had hair as red as her anger, but her moods were mercurial. Now the forest fire of her rage burned out and the tears that flowed from her eyes, her racking sobs, represented the quenching rainstorm of regret and despair. She again sprang to her feet, but this time instead of attacking her boyfriend she leapt into his arms and straddled him with her sexy legs. Shit Free was bleeding from the runnels that she had raked across the side of his face, but he immediately acquired a goofy, erotically inebriated grin and collapsed onto a barstool with The Bike in his blue-jean-clad lap, she straddling him with her naked legs and with her arms now wrapped around his neck. She buried her face in his shoulder and blubbered: "Oh, shit, Shit, I'm sorry. I'm so, so sorry. I swear to God I'm sorry. I know you hate that hip-hop shit but you weren't around and the Internet jukebox was there and I guess I just succumbed to Satan's apple."

He ran a hand through her fiery red hair and with the other he stroked her back, meanwhile bringing her in closer to him so that her crotch was above his. He rode The Bike, but sometimes The Bike rode him. He gave her ass in the cutoffs a squeeze and then squeezed a thigh and murmured into her ear, "Don't worry about it, baby doll, we all make mistakes. Now your Daddy Man has done shot out that devil jukebox and removed all temptation. Like Adam in the Garden woulda set that bitch Eve straight and snatched the apple from her hand 'efore she coulda ever ate it and sent everthin' to holy hell. All's forgiven. Course you been a bad girl and later when we get home I'll have to put ya over my knee, pull down your cut-offs and panties, if ya even have panties on, and give ya a spankin'." He reached down around and gave her ass another squeeze. Then with the flat of her hand he smacked the bottom of her thigh and that gorgeous roll of patriotic, American corn-fed flesh jiggled seductively. It jiggled and she giggled and then they began necking, tongue kissing, while the Gang watched with their own tongues hanging down nearly to the floor.

Shit Free had no problem with riding The Bike in public, or The Bike riding him — they'd done it before, indeed right here in this very bar — but somehow he wasn't in the mood just now. He was feeling ornery. He kept thinking about that fag in the gully he'd executed. It annoyed him to think that the wrong kind of people might be creeping into town. Yankees. Liberals. He peeled The Bike off of him and set her aright on her platforms. He gave her ass a smack and told her to go sit in a corner and be quiet. "Yes, Daddy," she said meekly, and clopped off, ass sashaying as she went. She plunked her ass down on a stool and crossed those hot legs of hers but kept her lip zipped like a good girl.

The Gang was abuzz with talk of Idaho sesech. Boris was an anarchist. Milton was an anarcho-libertarian. Roderick was an Ayn Rand Objectivist. Red Dave was a Socialist. Their contentious points of view always cooked up a nice bubbling broth of conflict, which is what made The Gang such lively companions. Nine-tenths of the time Shit Free did not understand one-tenth of what these goobers were talking about, but he felt deep affection for all of 'em in his slightly retarded and drooling homicidal way. He regarded The Gang as a band of brothers and if need be he'd die for 'em sure as shit. Even that filthy Commie Red Dave.

Sam served Shit a pitcher of Gutbuster beer and Shit joined "the politicians," as he liked to call this subset of The Gang, around a broad oak table as they argued.

"There is no such thing as 'anarcho-libertarianism,'" the bearded Boris insisted, addressing the lanky and laconic Milton, who annoyingly spoke in impenetrable verse but at least knew how to make money, a talent that Shit Free envied because he could not emulate it. Milton had a financial stake in the local Walmart, which had put all the family-owned stores of Whitely, Idaho, out of business, and had caused the local unemployment rate to skyrocket, but which also offered useless crap twenty or thirty percent cheaper than could be obtained locally, which would have allowed folks to "save money and live better" if only they had jobs and money. Milton could afford to sit around the Drink Here Bar on a morning such as this one, April 15, 2015, because he was wealthy and did not need to punch a clock. Most of the rest of the government-hating gang could afford to drink early and often because they were on welfare, Shit Free among them. Of course they had other ways of making money, none of 'em legal. "True anarchism," Boris announced, banging down his beer mug, "does not tolerate private property. We've been round and round on this, Milty. Your 'anarcho-libertarianism' is a bastardization of concepts, an impossible chimera, like mating a dog and a cat and expecting to get a catdog or a dogcat. It don't work. If you favor private property, you are not a goddamned anarchist."

Milton always spoke in the verse of the poet that shared his name, reciting it by heart but altering it strategically to serve his own ends. He had cleverly (or clumsily, depending on your point of view) recast Paradise Lost in such a way that God was the Invisible Hand, Satan was Marx and the apple in the Garden was a welfare state handout. He now stated:

> *"Th' infernal Marx; he it was, whose guile*
> *Stirred up with Envy and Revenge, deceiv'd*
> *The Mother of Mankind, what time his Pride*
> *Had cast him out from Heav'n, with all his Host*
> *Of Revolutionaries, by whose aid aspiring*
> *To set himself in Glory above his Peers,*
> *He trusted to have equal'd the most High,*
> *If he oppos'd; and with ambitious aim*
> *Against the Throne of the Invis'ble Hand*
> *Rais'd impious War in Heav'n and Battle proud*
> *With vain attempt. Him the Almighty Hand*
> *Hurld headlong flaming from th' Ethereal Skie*
> *With hideous ruine and combustion down*
> *To bottomless perdition, there to dwell*
> *In Admantine Chains and penal Fire,*
> *Who durst defie th' Invisible of Hand."*

Red Dave, the socialist, banged down his beer mug. He was sixty-eight years old and a transplanted New York City Jew. A widower, he had come to Idaho in his declining years to escape the big-city rat race and his two sons, who were failures. They had disappointed Red Dave by becoming wealthy Wall Street traders. But he had also moved here with the idea of proselytizing Red State Idaho to make it a Red State in the traditional sense: a socialist enclave, a *red* state. So far, he had spectacularly failed and once had nearly been lynched.

"Anarchism and Libertarianism are both stupid," Dave insisted. "The first because it believes that collective self-governance is wrong, even though it's not possible to exist without some form of government. Socialists like me want government from the bottom up, not the top down, with the workers controlling the means of production. Libertarianism is stupid because ... well, do I even need to say why Libertarianism is stupid, Milton? What you really advocate, perhaps without knowing it, is state corporate fascism: the defense of money and property rather than ordinary workers."

Roderick, the Randian Objectivist, believed that everyone in the bar was a second-hander. Despite his insults, the gang put up with him because he had inherited a large sum of money and he often bought the Gang a round of drinks, but only after lecturing them on the economic theories of Ludwig von Mises and on the Austrian School and the gold standard, eye-glazing monologues that the Gang put up with because they were perpetually thirsty. The Gang treated Roderick like the proverbial crazy aunt in the attic. Roderick said that he bought the drinks not because he was an altruist, but in his own self-interest: Getting the Gang sauced, he believed without evidence, would sooner or later make them more amenable to

Objectivist ideology. Roderick dreamed of recruiting The Gang to form a real-world Galt's Gulch. But first he would have to get them drunk, especially Red Dave. Roderick had a dollar sign tattooed on his ass.

"Sam!" Roderick snapped in the voice of a master summoning his butler, or maybe his pet dog. "A pitcher of Gutbuster. It's on me. You're welcome."

Sam brought the pitcher but Roderick did not tip him because he did not believe in altruism. He also felt that tips encouraged a unfortunate dependency in the hired help. Roderick was on welfare too, but he rationalized his mooching on the grounds that until a perfect sateless state of affairs existed, true capitalism could not exist. Until it existed, he thought, one must get by as one can. The fact that he had inherited a sizable sum did not dissuade him from bilking the state. He rationalized that by taking public funds that he did not need, he would demonstrate to the moocher class the bankruptcy of the welfare state and hence speed its inevitable demise. He worshiped the Invisible Hand the way that theists worship the Invisible God.

The talk turned to secesh.

"Do you really think," Boris demanded, "that the federal government is going to let the Red States go without a fight? Any more than it let the Old Confederacy go? And this time a Civil War will be short and sweet. The Blue States have the economic might, the military might, most of the industrial might, everything."

"There's no tyrant Lincoln this time, either," Roderick pointed out. "Just that weakling Obama."

Shit Free didn't bother with a mug. He picked up the pitcher of Gutbuster and guzzled away a third of it, slammed it down on the tabletop, belched, wiped beer suds from his lips, which were scarring over from the cuts he had given himself with broken bottle shards earlier, snatched his pistol out of a holster slung around his jeans and slammed the gun down on the center of the table, the same gun that he had used to assassinate the Internet jukebox. "Guns," he grunted. "The gummint's got guns but we got guns too. That's what the Second Amendment is all about. This time we can wage guerrilla war, if necessary."

Milton said,

Say first, for the Hand hides nothing from thy view
Nor the deep Tract of Hell, say first what cause
Mov'd our Grand Parents in that happy No State,
Favour'd of the Hand so highly, to fall off
From their Creator, and transgress his Will
For one restraint, Lords of the World besides?
Who first seduc'd them to that fowl revolt?
Th' infernal Marx; he it was, whose guile
Stird up with Envy and Revenge, deceiv'd
The Mother of Mankinde.

The others felt that Milton's contribution was off the point. What they all really wanted to do, secesh or no secesh, was overthrow the government in Washington, though they wanted to do so for different reasons. All were randy for rebellion. They had a hard-on for havoc.

"Let's form a Posse Comitatus," Shit Free said, gesticulating with enthusiasm. It had taken him a long time to learn those two words and memorize their meaning.

The others looked at him dubiously. Red Dave shook his white-maned, hoary head.

"Drive to Washington, and overthrow the gummint." Shit Free aimed his pistol at the ceiling and pulled the trigger. BANG!

Outside it had started raining, and now the roof

leaked.

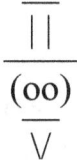

President Obama gazed out of the windows of the Oval Office. The April tree boughs bloomed with greenery, and birds twittered in them. Sunlight, filtered through the branches, streamed down through the panes and illumined the office, which was painted and appointed in reassuring middle-of-the-road middlebrow compromise colors: Beige dominated. But the chirping did not quite supersede the angry chants coming from the Mall, and the roars of maniacal glee at the presentation of Cyrus Clone (Cyclone) who, his moon face projected on large screens, ranted and raved from a secret bunker in the desuetude of the Old Confederacy, although actually Clone was speaking from a studio in Burbank, California, and was a gay man and failed actor named Elvis Kandor who was happily married to his devoted spouse, John Caswell.

Obama leaned forward, shoulders hunched, and lowered his head. It was a classic pose of thoughtfulness, the slumped shoulders suggesting the burden of responsibility that weighed upon the aging leader whose once sable-black hair had gone baby-powder white during his tour of duty in office. Obama posed while his official photographer snapped a photo for the ages. It had been seven years since Change. Now a new Change was aborning, a Cyclone of rebellion sweeping out of the Red States, red with anger. For the second time in its history, the Union was splitting apart, the land masses of its incompatible traditions and ideologies crashing and grinding along the fault lines of history. The last time that this had happened, James Buchanan was the president, with the storied Abraham Lincoln waiting in the wings. Buchanan dithered while the union dissolved, and Obama was keenly aware of history's judgment on the only bachelor (and probably gay) president: You flunk, sir. Sit in the corner with a dunce cap on your head. Forever.

In ten minutes, the president was scheduled to meet with his cabinet in the Cabinet Room around the large, elliptical mahogany table that was a gift from Richard Nixon.

Therefore it was time.

The president sat down behind The Resolution Desk. He opened a drawer.

Inside were his beloved Mr. Spock ears.

He put them on. The pointed ears covered his own, and were held in place by a string that went around his head.

He proceeded pointy-eared to the Cabinet room. The president's photographer rolled his eyes and did not take pictures of the president wearing his Mr. Spock ears. Such photos were forbidden, and only the president's inner sanctum, sworn to secrecy, knew about his Spock imposture.

```
      __
      ||
      __
     (oo)
      __
      V
```

"Look, let's cut the bullpucky here, sir," an indignant Officer Rob Boyle snapped at Abraham Lincoln. "D'ya think you're fooling anyone? Pretending never to have seen a laptop before? I know your game. You're an Abe

Lincoln impersonator pretending to be the real Abraham Lincoln risen from the dead after one hundred fifty years. What's it all about? Is it some kind of, ah, I guess they call it performance art? Or is this some secret reality TV show? Are their hidden cameras? What's your game, sir?"

The idealistic young police officer could not abide a haggard, filthy, reeking Abraham Lincoln who spoke in a voice like fingernails raking across a blackboard and told raunchy tales about shitting in outhouses and shagging whores on the prairie. Boyle was an Evangelical Christian, and this was like finding out that Christ was a boozer and derelict who enjoyed gay sex with his disciples.

Lincoln turned his attention from the laptop and gazed levelly and coolly and silently and disconcertingly at Boyle, his lazy left eye drifting up into its window-shade lid. A fly circled around Lincoln's haggard head, his hair preternaturally askew. Boyle again felt a chill. He was suddenly convinced anew that his man, whoever he was, was dangerous.

"Young man," the sixteenth president of the United States drawled, in a drawn-out and kindly voice, a crinkly, lopsided grin suddenly creasing his face like a watermelon rind and his gray eyes again dancing with mischief. "Tell me, are you a prayin' man?"

"Of course I am!"

"Well, I am too, son. Problem is, when I pray, the Lord thinks I'm jokin'."

Officer Sully Stark had been drinking a can of Coke, and now he spewed some of it out through his nostrils and mouth with a snort of laughter. Lincoln hee-hawed with him, and slapped his bony, black-clad knee in delight. Officer Boyle got red in the face, but held his tongue. Sully tapped Abe's elbow and drew his attention back to the laptop. The basset-faced officer whose whole career had been a concatenation of one banality after another felt alive for the first time in years, maybe in his entire life. He was irrationally convinced that this man really was Abraham Lincoln. And he, Sully Stark, was pleased to introduce this towering historic figure of the 19th century to the 21st century. Until Boyle's priggish interruption, he had been giving Lincoln a laptop tutorial. Now the lesson resumed.

"This is the track pad and the is the click pad, Mr. President. That's the cursor."

Lincoln moved the cursor around on the screen. "How long have I been asleep?" he asked.

"A hundred fifty years, sir," Sully said.

"Rip Van Winkle," the president muttered after a long pause. "How, exactly, did I fall asleep? Why did I wake to find myself buried underground, like a dead man?"

"You *were* a dead man, sir," Sully said. "What's the last thing you remember, before waking up?"

Lincoln cogitated.

"Ford's Theater," he said, with dawning awareness. "I was with Molly. We were watching ... Our American Cousin." Lincoln knitted his shaggy black brows and then retrieved from his restored memory, "'You sockdologizing old mantrap!' That was the last thing I recall hearing from the stage. Then I think I heard a loud BANG. Then I woke up underground and broke through the earth above me."

Stark filled him in on John Wilkes Booth.

Lincoln gazed down at the laptop screen. He was silent in contemplation. Then he muttered, "Man is not the only animal who labors; but he is the only one who improves his workmanship." After a long, thoughtful pause, the president asked, "What is the state of the union? I trust it is still intact and eternal, as I struggled to make it?"

The officers traded glances. Officer Boyle continued to look rueful and offended. Stark explained to Lincoln how to launch a browser. They navigated to newyorktimes. com where the 16th president of the United States, who had signed the Emancipation Proclamation and pushed through the 13th Amendment ending slavery, saw a jpeg of President Barack Obama and learned that the Union was again on the brink of breaking up.

Stark noted Lincoln's astounded expression and said, "Welcome to the asylum, sir. Or should I say, welcome back to it."

CHAPTER 3
WORLD BEATER

"They let you smoke here?"

"Don't tell the Health Department, the police or the Nanny State. We're underground, remember."

Alexander World looked on with ill-concealed distaste as Amanda Clocker drew in a deep drag from the death coffin that she held between middle and index finger. His distaste was reserved for the cigarette and the inhalation, however. The puckering of her lips as she inhaled was on the other side of town of distaste. It looked as if she were giving the cigarette a blow job.

They had a secluded table in an intimate corner of the club. He had never been here, but people recognized World. They were cordoned off and given privacy, as well as the doting genuflections of a wait staff avid to refill drinks, to provide food and sup and to light illicit cigarettes. Amanda Clocker had lighted her own.

"You really should quit," World said, immediately regretting the prissy words that flowed out of his mouth without his consent. Undaunted, those nerd words, with a mind of their own, pressed on in lecture: "Smokers have five times the mortality from lung cancer than non-smokers. And that is not even to mention the peril of emphysema, heart disease, stroke, tooth decay and even blindness." His eyes wandered down to her cleavage, exposed by the clinging scarlet dress with the plunging neckline that she wore. Then his eyes wandered back up to those florid lips, still kissably puckered as she exuded smoke that jetted toward the fluorescent ceiling and then dissolved in chaotic curlicues in the ghoulish light.

"I like to gamble, Alex," Amanda Clocker said huskily, setting the cigarette down in an ashtray on the white linen tablecloth. His eyes crawled down to the filter, and he noticed lipstick on it. "It's like playing a chess game with death."

"How very Ingmar Bergman," he muttered, now disgusted by his erudition in addition to his prissiness. Would a 23-year-old even know about The Seventh Seal? Amanda was twenty-three years old and he was thirty, not a great age difference, yet somehow he felt as if he and his top quantum computer programmer were separated by eons, and that they might as well have been communing on opposite sides of the Grand Canyon rather than on opposite sides of a small table in an intimate nook in an underground club that let you smoke if you were important enough.

"I can program Hickenlooper's Dreamworld, Alex."

"Are you sure? It's the biggest challenge we've ever faced. I'm dubious."

"I can give the man what he wants. I can teach it round, or I can teach it flat. I can teach it old, or I can teach it young."

"Excuse me?"

"Old academic joke. About a man applying for a position teaching geography in Texas."

"You're really smart, Amanda. I always underestimate you, to my regret I suppose. Did you understand the Bergman reference? The Seventh Seal?"

"Of course. You should give me a raise for that alone."

"Done. My wife is pregnant."

"What?"

"My wife is pregnant."

"Congrats."

"You don't sound too happy about it. Same way she told me that I didn't sound too happy about it when she told me about it."

"Are you happy about it?"

"I'm delirious with ecstasy. What about you?"

"Why does my opinion matter?"

"I guess it doesn't. I just … I … well … " His words trailed off in a train wreck. He was sixteen years old again in the computer cave at his high school, with the pens in the pen protector in the pocket of his white shirt leaking and big horn-rimmed glasses set awkwardly upon the bridge of his too-big nose. Skinny and shy, the butt of jokes. Scared to death of girls. Tongue-tied. Sometimes Lifestyle stories in the local papers talked about how being nerdy was the New Cool, and how computer programming today was as hot as being a high school quarterback had been a generation ago. False. High school never changes. It was, is, and always will be a torture chamber for the intelligent. High school is for the stupid, who constitute the bulk of humanity. The worst part, he thought, is that high school never ends.

She sipped her martini. He nursed his Coke.

"You should try something stronger," she advised.

"I don't drink."

"Don't drink. Don't smoke. What are your vices, Alex?"

"I don't have any."

"Really? None at all?"

"Do I? Should I?"

"You're a pusher."

"Excuse me?"

"Pushing this drug on poor Mr. Hickenlooper.

Giving him his dream. That's your vice. You're a pusher."

"Granting his wish, giving him his Dreamworld, is like giving him a drug?"

"Sure, but there's nothing wrong with drugs. Whatever gets you through the night. Or the life." She sipped her martini and inhaled her smoke. She replaced the cigarette in the ashtray. The filter was scarlet from her lips. It was dark and reddish-brown, like menstrual blood.

When World lifted his Coke to his lips his hand visibly shook and the ice rattled in the drink. He set it down unsteadily.

"Anything wrong, Alex?"

"We need to get down to business, Amanda," World said, affecting as best he could a brusque tone of voice while trying to tear his eyes away from the cleavage that elliptically bisected her milky breasts. "Hickenlooper is offering us a fortune. This is the biggest project that Dreamworlds has ever had. If we make this work, there is no limit. Not even the sky."

"May I see the check?"

He showed it to her.

His eyes crawled down under the table, where she had crossed her legs. Her skirt was so short that her thighs were on full display. She did not wear nylons.

"Were you a nerd in high school, Alex?" Her question caught him off guard. With the help of a doting retinue of PR agents he had craftily massaged his biography for public consumption, but the truth always leaked out. "Yes," he blurted out, intending to say No.

"Do you love your wife?"

"No." He had intended to say Yes.

A heavy silence hung between them as she looked at him hungrily with her slanted green eyes and wanton lips. A shiver passed up the nape of his neck as he felt the toe of her high heel shoe running up his pant cuff. He gulped. Self-consciously he said, "Weightlifting. That's how I got a hard body. Skinny as a rail in high school." He chuckled mirthlessly.

"I like hard bodies. "

"And I like soft bodies." He had not intended to say that, either.

There was a moment of awkward silence — awkward on his part. Then World abruptly asked her: "Do you know what the Dark Enlightenment is, Amanda?"

"No."

He told her.

"I Googled 'Dark Enlightenment,'" he said with a fatuous grin. "That's how I found out. Homer Hickenlooper tipped me off to it."

She stared numbly at him. For the first time it was he, not she, who was on top. It bucked him up.

But then her numb expression resolved back into predatory sultriness. It seemed she was pretending that he had not said what he had said.

Amanda Clocker reached into her purse and fetched a set of keys. She dangled them from the ring, between thumb and index finger, and they moved from side to side like a hypnotist's watch. World's eyes moved from side to side in dumb pursuit. Then he watched, mesmerized, as she set the keys down on the table next to the check.

"A copy of the keys to my apartment, Alex," she said. "Use these keys, and Mr. Hickenlooper will be well pleased. Don't use them ... well, maybe he won't be pleased by his Dreamworld. Maybe he won't be pleased by it at all. If a rich man isn't pleased, it will destroy our reputation. Remember, we do have competitors now. We've got hackers stealing our source code. Dreamworlds won't be a monopoly forever."

Now he stared at her.

"Use it or lose it, Alex." She stabbed out her cigarette. Then she abruptly rose and left the club, high heels clicking on the floor. World watched her legs with lust.

He decided to stop being a teetotaler and to get drunk by himself at the bar. He tipped the bartender generously to keep his area clear of gawkers and autograph seekers. He was alone, a quiet island in a clamorous ocean of noise, a lonely figure brooding over apartment keys and a gin and tonic. He took a sip, grimaced, swallowed with difficulty and set the glass down. The alcohol went to his head almost at once. How can people drink shit like this? he wondered. The bar area was lined with high-def, flat-screen TVs, and looking up, he saw that Fox News was on. "Could you turn up the volume?" he asked the bartender, who did, but the voices on-screen could not drown out the clamorous jabber of the crowd, which, invading his ears with vile voices, ratified an old saying that now returned to him: "Great minds discuss ideas, average minds discuss events, small minds discuss people." The mob around him was discussing some events, but mostly they were discussing people. They certainly were not discussing ideas. He was back in high school. He looked up with disinterest at the TV screen, vaguely trying to recall what he had hoped to hear on the news. Fortunately, although the voices of the announcers could not be heard above the hubbub, the broadcast was close-captioned for the hearing impaired, so he keenly followed the stream of words as a trader on Wall Street might follow the stock market ticker.

On the station whose motto was, "We Report, You Decide," a commentator was enthusing about a new video showing a visit to heaven. A private consortium had allegedly built "a rocket ship to the other side," and had landed the heavenly equivalent of astronauts — thananauts, they were called, derived from Thanatos, the personification of death — in the celestial imperium, the domain of Jesus. The video showed grainy footage of what appeared to be the Shroud of Turin blown up to ludicrous proportions, with several men who seemed to be dressed in Hazmat suits gamboling about and genuflecting in front of it. The video was laughably fake, like the shroud itself, a clumsy forgery, so bad that World became inspired and decided that Dreamworlds ought to be building virtual Heavens for the devout. Following the close-captioned ticker, he watched with incredulity as the Fox TV announcer prattled on about the first visit of living people to the Afterworld, and how the private consortium, Thananautics, was also planning to land some intrepid explorers on Hell's fiery shore to demonstrate, via video, the ominous fate that awaited nonbelievers. Ad break. World felt a spasm of contempt, his familiar contempt for mankind. The old familiar existential loneliness that he had first experienced around age five, when he had first contemplated suicide, ran through him, slithered through his guts like a plague of snakes. Loneliness. There followed some other news reports about how terrible the president was, how the United States was hurtling toward secession and a second Civil War, and then World's eyes widened and his ears pricked when the report shifted to what he had wanted to know more about, but had forgotten about: the CNN report that he had read on his laptop that morning after his meeting with Homer Hickenlooper, about the robbery of Lincoln's tomb.

Nursing his drink, one elbow propped up on the bar top and chin cradled in his palm, World followed the grave-robbing report with mingled fascination and disgust. Local officials speculated that the robbery had something to do with impending secesch. Lincoln's moldering beanstalk form, they suspected, had been stolen by one side or the other to serve as a symbol of something or other. But then the report shifted to a news conference from Springfield, Illinois. World looked agog at the screen.

Abraham Lincoln looked back down at him.

Tall, gaunt, sunken-cheeked, sad-eyed, disheveled. Uncouth and unkempt. That homely, leathery cadaver. Unmistakable. And lonely. This was not, World felt certain, Daniel Day Lewis portraying Lincoln. This was not a Lincoln impersonator. This was Abraham Lincoln. The sixteenth president of the United States sat there big (and tall) as life beside a basset-faced cop, and faced a small group of local reporters. The cop spoke first, and World followed the ticker that scrolled his scarcely believable or conceivable words across the bottom of the HDTV screen. World was so rapt that he forgot to be rapt. He failed to read all the words but key words, like words typed into a search engine, leapt out at him: "Rose from the grave … walking along the roadside … Learning about cars, personal computers, television, modern times and recent history ... quick study ... There's no doubt about it, ladies and gentlemen: God restored this man to us, from the past, to fix the problems of *our* times, because they so closely mirror the problems of *his* times. That's my conviction. The hand of God is behind the resurrection of Abraham Lincoln, the 16th president of the United States."

World abandoned his plan to get smashed for the first time, leapt off his barstool and bolted out of the club, pushing past the jostling mob of morons that infested it. Once out into the relative quiet of the street, dusk coming on, he pulled out his cellphone and surfed to Foxnews. com. He wanted to not just see, but hear, what would happen next. He wanted to *hear* the voice of Lincoln.

As soon as Lincoln began speaking, World felt funny in the gut. Amanda Clocker had once programmed a virtual Lincoln for a man who wanted to relive the Civil War. Watching and listening to Lincoln speak, World was convinced that this man in Springfield, Illinois, was in fact Clocker's creation. The voice was identical. A virtual clone of Lincoln, courtesy of Clocker. The idea filled him with foreboding, but lent credibility to a terrible idea that he had long toyed with: Suppose there is no real difference between our so-called real world, and the virtual worlds that Dreamworlds builds for wealthy clients? He recalled his lecture to Hickenlooper about the Matrix, Descartes' demon, et al, and now he soberly confronted the possibility that he had long feared: that Dreamworlds' virtual creations would somehow escape, like genies from bottles, like evil from Pandora's Box, and spread their smoke among the mirrors and labyrinths of what we are pleased, intersubjectively, to call reality. Smoke and mirrors and labyrinths. And Amanda Clocker, who had offered to serve Hickenlooper in exchange for some servicing from Alex World. World snatched the keys that she had copied for him from his pocket and looked at them for a long time. From between his thumb and index finger they dangled like a talisman, a symbol charged with myth and meaning, like the Cross, the Crescent and Star, or the Star of David. Like the Double Helix of biology or like the Wave Function, the sign of advanced quantum computing that Dreamworlds had pioneered. Just as he was struggling to overcome the sheer idiocy of likening the keys to Amanda Clocker's apartment to the icons of religion and science, his attention was arrested by Abe's tinny rustic voice. He heard Lincoln say: "In my position it is somewhat important that I should not say any foolish things." With that Lincoln broke off the news conference, rose, bowed stiffly, and then loped out of the room, putting on his stovepipe hat as he did. Reporters yelled questions after him but he was gone, the last glimpse of him his tall shadow rising and bobbing along the wall before it too was gone.

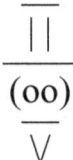

In the Cabinet room, around the large elliptical desk gifted by Richard Nixon, President Obama, wearing his Spock ears, had convened his cabinet.

"Captain Kirk, as always, is absent," Obama began the meeting as he always did, evoking covert eye rolls from several advisers, including the vice president. "So logically, I am in charge."

The cabinet members waited. Some nervous coughing and shuffling of papers broke the weighty silence. President Obama continued:

"It is simply illogical that our country is breaking up," Obama fretted, while maintaining a reasonable tone of voice.

"What does logic have to do with governance or history, Mr. President?" the vice president inquired, adopting a jocular and inoffensive mien. He was plotting his own campaign to succeed Obama, making it necessary to placate him, but he also had to keep an eye on the Hillary Machine that was stirring to life, less than a year from the Iowa caucuses. "History is a chronicle of the irrational."

"Illogical, Joe. Explain yourself."

The veep searched for something to say. Finally he fetched from memory a quote from the novel 2666, by the character Benno von Archimboldi: "History, which is a simple whore, has no decisive moments but is a proliferation of instants, brief interludes that vie with one another in monstrousness."

The president cogitated. He had been playing with a pencil between his fingers and now, betraying an inner tension he had hoped to disguise, he broke it in half. In the silence of the cabinet room, a silence only vaguely interrupted by the distant shouts of the secesh rally at the Mall, the breaking of the pencil sounded like an ax hitting the trunk of a tree.

The vice president reached under the table and produced a six pack of Gutbuster beer. He cracked the tab of one of the cans. The other officials looked on nervously as the beer foamed out of the top of the opened can.

Holding up the six-pack by its plastic rungs, the veep looked around the room and asked jocularly, "Brewskis? Anyone?"

President Obama drummed the two pieces of the snapped pencil on the polished tabletop like tiny yellow drumsticks. He peered soberly at the beer and said, "Joe, beer is not appropriate in the Cabinet Room. I believe we have discussed this delicate matter before, in some detail."

The veep suddenly understood what Obama's problem had always been. No one feared him. And this meant that the veep didn't have to fear him, either, to advance his own political fortunes. He took a swig.

"Bugger off, sir," Joe Biden said with a jaunty FDR grin. "You're a lame duck. And I do mean lame. I may be irreverent, but you're *irrelevant*. In fact, your name will appear only a few more times in this novel, toward the end of it, and not flatteringly." Biden belched. Then he added: "And your Spock ears are ridiculous, sir. I mean, really, dude. Ring, ring! Clue phone! Answer it for once, for fuck sake. Take a clue-by-four upside the head."

 END BOOK ONE

\<Interregnum\>

An interregnum (plural interregna or interregnums) is a period of discontinuity or "gap" in a government, organization or social order. Archetypically, it was the period of time between the reign of one monarch and the next (coming form Latin inter-, "between" plus regnum, "reign," (from rex, regis, "king") and the concepts of interregnum and regency therefore overlap. — Wikipedia

In the history of the U.S. presidency, the two most difficult interregnums were 1860-61, when the outgoing president, James Buchanan, and the incoming chief executive, Abraham Lincoln; and 1932-33, between the lame duck Herbert Hoover and the regnant-to-be, FDR. In the first case, the nation was falling apart as state after state seceded during the power vacuum that lasted from the November election until the March 4, 1861, inauguration of Lincoln. In the latter case, the Great Depression was deepening to its nadir and banks were closing like falling dominoes nationwide during the gap between the election and FDR's March 4 inauguration. In 1933 the 20th Amendment was ratified, specifying that the presidential inauguration should take place on January 20 of the new year following the November election, the goal being to avoid the prolonged and perilous power vacuums of the interregnums described above.

April 25, 2015, ten days after the reappearance of Lincoln

"Dragonflies, Mr. Kandor."
"Dragonflies?"

"Dragonflies."

In his suite of offices in a San Francisco high-rise overlooking Market Street, Homer Hickenlooper, real-estate magnate and daft recluse, took out of a drawer in his desk a glass case in which was a dead dragonfly impaled upon a pin, the point of which was fastened into a floor lined with cotton. The specimen had a wingspan of nearly a foot. Elvis Kandor, aka Cyrus Clone or Cyclone, swallowed with difficulty. Those crystalline wings, the massive compound eye orbs, the long delicate legs and elongated midsection ... the bug made him shudder. It was really big.

"Kind of scary," he offered.

"You think so? Most people think they are cute. Like ladybugs."

"Looks nasty to me, Mr. Hickenlooper."

"Nature's drone, Mr. Clone."

"Kandor, please. Thanks. What do you mean, 'nature's drone,' Mr. Hickenlooper?"

"As I'm sure you know, sir, drones are big technology right now. Remotely controlled, they hover, dip, dive and attack in enemy foreign lands, and even conduct surveillance here in the United States. They are predators, and bad guys are their prey. Increasingly they are programmed with chips that give them, as it were, independence of thought. The goal is to have intelligent drones that can ferret out and exterminate the Bad Guys without any input from remote controllers."

"What's this got to do with anything, Mr. Hickenlooper? What does it, for instance have to do with —" he nodded squeamishly at the well-preserved dragonfly corpse — "that ungodly thing?"

"Ungodly! If only you knew, sir. The dragonfly is nature's greatest hunter. Its kill rate is 95 percent. Contrast that with the fearsome lion, which kills only roughly a quarter of the prey that it pursues. Sharks rise to fifty percent."

Kandor stared with growing unease at the monster in the glass case.

"Their compound eyes can see all the way around their head. They can fly up to thirty miles an hour. They can fly up, down, backwards and forwards, and they can operate their wings independently. Most impressively of all, they can think top-down: Like a man at a party who singles out a friend and focuses his attention on that person while shunting aside the competing hubbub of the crowd, the dragonfly can choose to home in on a victim — a fly, say — out of a crowd of flies, a victim that promises the most nourishment. The prey. The enemy."

"What's your point, sir?"

"I have a lot of money, and I choose to invest it wisely. Right now I am investing it in a certain company that shall remain nameless — it is on the so-called budgetary Black Book of the Pentagon — to which the military has subcontracted a study of dragonflies."

"The Pentagon is studying dragonflies, Mr. Hickenlooper? Why?"

"Sir, do you believe in God?"

"I — I don't know that question has to do with, uh ... anything."

The Homer Hickenlooper who had been so shy and deferential, so doddering and pathetic, in his meeting with Alexander the Great, now brimmed with inner confidence, and his aging body thrummed with tension, a good kind of tension that made him almost visibly young again. The tension of alertness and adrenaline and youth. Conviction. Certitude.

"The dragonfly, Mr. Kandor, is a precision killer

whose abilities far exceed that of our drones, which were so precisely and painstakingly engineered. The Pentagon people want to know what makes them work so good, so that they can adapt those abilities for our drones. America's finest minds have spent years making and upgrading drones, which do a good job to a certain extent. But they are nowhere near as good as nature's drones, the dragonflies, which have a 95 percent kill rate, compared with America's engineered drones, which miss their targets almost half the time while also piling up a vast number of innocent bodies, what the Pentagon calls Collateral Damage. Why do you suppose that is, sir?"

"Why do I suppose what is?"

"Why is the advanced human mind, with its plans and intentions, inferior to mindless nature? Why does nature, with no intention at all, produce a dragonfly with a 95 percent kill rate, while the Pentagon, with the best minds in existence, produces a drone with a kill rate under fifty percent along with Collateral Damage? How is that possible?"

Kandor found nothing to say. So Hickenlooper said it for him.

"The idea that dragonflies were produced by a blind process of descent with modification and random genetic drift, also called evolution, is total and tragic nonsense, sir. How can mindlessness produce a more efficient and ruthless killer than mind? The inference is inescapable: All life is a product of intelligent design, and the reasonable conclusion is that the designer is a supernatural person with a special interest in humans. His name is Jesus. Wouldn't you agree, sir?"

"No."

"I invest," Hickenlooper reiterated. "Right now I'm also investing my future in a Dreamworld. Just in case I can't make my dreams come true in this world."

"A Dreamworld, Mr. Hickenlooper? You mean —"

"Alexander the Great. Yes."

"What is your Dreamworld, sir?"

"It's a world in which Goldwater was elected president in 1964. It's a world of good Christian believers, in which Intelligent Design is taught in schools, with the dragonfly as a paradigmatic example of the mind of God. It's a world of top-down authority, where the wealthy are given the tax cuts and deference due to them, rather than the scorn and Socialism of the current gang in Washington. A world of conservative economics and values, of unerring and pitiless Dragonflies that kill our enemies both internal and external. Kill them with extreme prejudice."

"What has this got to do with me, Mr. Hickenlooper? Why did you make this appointment with me? Did you intend to offer me something? A job, maybe?"

"Yes, Mr. Kandor, I've seen your Cy Clone Webcasts. Very impressive. Recently you had the mob at the Mall riled up into a lather. I like that. Those are my kind of people. And your Cy Clone is my kind of people."

"But surely you realize, sir, that Elvis Kandor and Cy Clone are two different people? My act is … well, an *act*. For the rubes."

"For what purpose, Mr. Kandor?"

"I'm sure you can guess, sir. The persona I sell makes money. It's very popular. But if it were only about money, I wouldn't pretend to be Cyclone, calling for the breakup of America, the second secession. I do it because I want to see the Red States peel off from the Blue States. I hate the Red States, and their values, and want to see them gone. I'm sure you can appreciate, sir, that this means that I hate *your* values. So, what is it that you want from me?"

"Just continue to do the same, only more of it.

Although our motives differ, our goals are the same: the breakup of America. In case that doesn't happen, I have taken out an insurance policy: My own Dreamworld. If America breaks up, I can choose between the real world and the Dreamworld."

"More of the same, only more of it? What do you mean?"

"I'll pay you a substantial sum to take your tour on the road, Mr. Kandor. Cyrus Clone. Cyclone, the wind out of the Old Confederacy. Gone with the wind? Back with the wind! The voice of vengeance and renewal. The Lost Cause. You shall revive it. You shall help, more than you have until now, to condition the public mind to accept the breakup of the United States and the revival of the Confederacy, and this time with the Rocky Mountain States attached. A new nation espousing the values to which I subscribe."

"I'm afraid I can't do that, Mr. Hickenlooper. You see, I'm *playacting*. It's fine to do that on the other side of a Webcam. It's like being on a Web site message board and pretending to be someone you are not: like a woman pretending to be a man or a man a woman. But then when you log out, you are, who you are. I can't possibly go physically public, as opposed to virtually or virally public, and pretend to be someone whom I'm not. It's like that guy going around impersonating Lincoln. Now *he's* an actor! He's got everyone eating out of the palm of his hand. Once, I wanted to be an actor. But I failed."

"And suppose, sir, I blew the whistle on your little Web scam, and revealed you for the trickster that you are? I know that you are married to another man, for example."

Kandor paused and regarded the magnate with bemusement. "What of it, sir? Are you seriously trying to blackmail me? Who cares if everyone found out who

I really am? In fact, my true identity is already common knowledge. Exposés about my true self are all over the Web: There have been exposés at Slate, Salon, Reddit, the Huffington Post ... "

Hickenlooper leaned back in his chair and waved his hand dismissively. "Of course, sir, understood, but the people who want to believe that you are the conservative firebrand Cyclone will believe it regardless of the facts that show otherwise; indeed even *because* the facts show otherwise. In the modern world, where knowledge is so easy to acquire via the Internet, everyone simply makes up his her own facts, and people believe that which they wish to believe, even when the belief is demonstrated to be empirically invalid."

"Then your apparent blackmail attempt against me is pointless, isn't it? I imagine you want a world with gays back in the closet, too. Don't you?"

"Of course. I can't stand you faggots. ... Well, I had hoped that you would succumb to blackmail. It would have been much cheaper for me. Instead, I'll buy you off." He wrote a check and presented it to Kandor/Cyclone, who looked at it agog.

"Will you do it?"

"Yes."

May 15, 2015, 2015, one month after the reappearance of Lincoln: an exchange on an unknown Internet message board

davidm

Those oldies, but goodies, remind me of you ...

Grant vs. Lee ... WTF? Hanky-panky in the War Department! Thaddeus Stevens tells Lincoln, during a discussion of the honesty of Simon Cameron, the new war secretary: "I don't believe he would steal a red-hot stove." Learning of this, Cameron demands that Stevens take it back. Stevens complies, telling Lincoln: "I believe I told you he would not steal a red-hot shoe. I will now take that back." ... OMG! Secession! "The civil war was never about slavery. It was about state's rights." ... From the Cornerstone speech of Alexander Stephens, the Confederate veep: "The Constitution, it is true, secured every essential guarantee to the institution while it should last, and hence no argument can be justly urged against the constitutional guarantees thus secured, because of the common sentiment of the day. Those ideas, however, were fundamentally wrong. They rested upon the assumption of the equality of races. This was an error. It was a sandy foundation, and the government built upon it fell when the storm came and the wind blew. Our new government is founded upon exactly the opposite idea; its foundations are laid, its cornerstone rests, upon the great truth that the negro is not equal to the white man; that slavery subordination to the superior race is his natural and normal condition. This, our new government, is the first, in the history of the world, based upon this grand physical, philosophical and moral truth."

Yes, boys and girls, Lincoln is back, and with him, history itself resumes! As Faulkner said, The past isn't dead. It isn't even past."

AW

Hello, all, I am a new member here, and I am Darkly Enlightened. You should be, too.

The emergence and rise of this person claiming to be Lincoln (for who in their right mind could believe him to be the real Lincoln — it is more apposite to suppose that he is a *virtual* Lincoln who has slipped the surly bonds of Cyberspace, and burst upon the real life as out of a 3D printer. Perhaps one day we shall *all* be reincarnated via 3D printing, which even now, in its nascent stages, can already produce guns, houses, horses and dreams. But I digress, and also I'm a little drunk. Sorry for drunk posting.)

Where was I? The emergence of Lincoln fills a jaded America with hope. Lincoln *is* America. In him, or his memory, we retrospectively cash out all our hopes for what America is, or should be, and what we should like ourselves to be: literate, open, liberal, egalitarian, believing in national self rule, believing in Democracy with a capital "D."

I used to believe these things myself, but I no longer do. I have experienced an epiphany. A dark epiphany.

In a flash of darkness, a black flash that shadowed rather than illumined my face, I discerned the truth. Lincoln said that "those who would deny freedom to others, deserve it not for themselves." But I saw in a black flash that this was wrong. Some deserve freedom and others do not. Democracy is mob rule. Better a kind of feudalism, or Plato's Republic, the rule of the wise, to produce a just society which must necessarily be based on hierarchies because all men are *not* created equal in any relevant sense. Certainly this supposed truth, as mooted by the founders, is *not* self-evident in any logical sense. I hold with Guillaume Faye, who calls for "the re-emergence of archaic configurations — pre-modern, inegalitarian and non-humanist, wedded to traditionalist religious beliefs coupled with — and this is the modern topper — a *techno-utopia* engineered by the best and the brightest who have blazed the trails of cyberspace. Perhaps you can guess who I am by the initials of my user name.

SadSack

Who the fuck is Guillaume Faye?

Jettison Jester

tl;dr

Windbag

OMFG! Breaking news, with video to come: The Paradise 72 Brigades Inc., the new Muslim terrorist transnational corporation that now controls two-thirds of the Middle East and claims to have acquired a worldwide string of banks and nuclear weapons, announces its fighters robbed Lincoln's grave, stole the corpse of the 16th president and is holding it for ransom!

Godel's Theorem

Frame pull linked below of video of Lincoln's corpse on its knees, a P72 black-clad fighter holding a carving knife to the neck of the corpse, with the following: "We will behead the corpse of Lincoln unless the infidel U.S. government of the Cross pays P72 $50 billion in ransom, via wire transfer to our accounts in the United Arab Emirates."

Failed Prophecy

WTF? Will the real Lincoln please stand up? (Well, not the corpse if the corpse is the real Lincoln; corpses can't stand.) Is the corpse real, or the guy going around calling himself Lincoln? What's the truth here?

Richard Rorty

[Postmodernism] affirms that whatever we accept as truth and even the way we envision truth are dependent on the community in which we participate ... There is no absolute truth: truth is relative to the community in which we participate.

May 15, 2015 (Later the same day; Springfield, Illinois)

"I know you. You're President Abraham Lincoln. I once saw you on a five-dollar bill, the first five dollars I ever earned."

Hortense Stark sat in an easy chair, propped up like a mummy, in the living room of the modest brick house that she shared with her husband, Sergeant Sullivan (Sully) Stark. There was also a live-in nurse to tend to Mrs. Stark while Sully was at work.

Lincoln was bowing gallantly toward her and extending a hand, after Stark had introduced her to Lincoln, saying, "Mommy, we're going to have a house guest for a while."

The nurse, a white-clad, sad-faced Haitian immigrant who spoke little but was dutiful and resolute, a woman accustomed to tragedy and despair, a devout Catholic who dutifully bore her Cross, pattered into the living room and took a hairbrush to Mrs. Stark's hair, a graying corona of frazzled split-ends that surrounded the ailing woman's blank and palsied face like a tatterdemalion halo. As she brushed the hair Lincoln continued to bow, hand extended, but Mrs. Stark sat with her hands composed on her lap in the folds of her bathrobe. Her eyes had fastened like pinpoints on the face of Lincoln, that beloved face from the first five dollars that she had ever earned a seeming eternity ago, but then they immediately lost their luster and acquired the appearance of two coins without embossments: just two blank discs of silver, staring stupidly outward at everlasting Nothing.

Lincoln creaked his old bones aright and withdrew

his hand while Stark watched his wife in amazement.

"I'm afraid she's almost gone, Mr. President. It's simply astounding that she recognized you. She no longer recognizes me, and I'm her husband."

"Call me Lincoln," Lincoln responded abstractly, taking in the demented woman still sitting bolt-upright in her chair while the Haitian nurse brushed Mrs. Stark's hair. "May I ask what ails her?"

"I think in your time, sir, they called it dementia. Now it's called Alzheimer disease."

Lincoln nodded somberly.

"She's lost her mind," Stark elaborated with a hitching breath, followed by a strangled sob. His shoulders violently shook, and he buried his face in his hands. Lincoln laid a long arm around those rounded shoulders and with touch alone, wordlessly comforted the cop. For a time, only Stark's sobs and the crackling of the hairbrush broke the painful silence.

"My first five dollars from the first paycheck I ever cashed," Mrs. Stark suddenly piped up, eyes coming to life again. "I worked as a maid in the Richmond home of the president of the Confederate States, Jefferson Davis."

"Mommy," Stark gently reprimanded his wife, fearing that she was deliberately insulting Lincoln, "your first job was as a clerk at a local printing firm. Besides, how could you have been paid with a five-dollar bill with Mr. Lincoln's face on it? In the first place, it would have been Confederate money; in the second place, Lincoln's face wasn't on a five-dollar bill until the twentieth century."

"Now I want to pee," the void-faced woman announced loudly with jarring candor unmediated by her disintegrating ego. A moment later there was a faint sizzling sound. Stark broke down anew, and Lincoln, clutching the sergeant's elbow, gently steered him away from the woman in the chair while the Haitian nurse brushed that brushfire of gray hair with redoubled ardor, as if by doing so she could wish away the mess that she would have to clean up.

The empty eyes of the woman in the chair drifted toward the picture window of the house, the drapery drawn back, the window looking out on a wide lawn, some elm trees and the road beyond.

The eyes again eerily changed into dark pinpoints of concentration, as lucidity briefly returned to the brain behind them.

What she saw was a big white truck pulling to a stop at the curb. The words FUNNY FARM were printed in black block letters on the side of the truck.

Some men dressed in white clambered out of it, holding huge butterfly nets and walking up to the front porch of the Stark estate.

"Oh, Mr. Lincoln," Hortense Stark sang out in the tenor notes of a chirping bird. "The men in the white coats have come to take you away. To the funny farm, where life is beautiful all the time."

The doorbell rang. Ding-Dong!

</Interregnum>

Book Two
The Fateful Lightning

Chapter One
Abe Has Come to Save the Day

Alexander World and Amanda Clocker lay entwined in bed, in a cyclone of sodden sheets.

She rolled on top him, growling. Her hand wandered down between his legs, and she seized his erect cock while he groped her ass. Their lips met, and they hungrily kissed while she pulled on his pud. He wrapped his arms around her and clung to her ferociously. They panted and slobbered, and then she mounted him. She straddled him and began to bounce her software up and down upon his hardware. Within moments both of them were saying O God O God O God like a repetitive Google search string and after the drumroll followed by the crescendo there was satiety, the two of them lying in each other's arms like spent search algorithms, panting as the fireworks faded. He ran his fingers through her long hair and she nestled her head on his hairy chest, moaning with ecstasy and biting and licking at his left nipple.

World's hand wandered over to the TV remote on the table next to their sodden fuck sack and he flicked it at the flat-screen TV on the opposite wall. Abraham Lincoln stared back at him. In full HD color.

"Look," he said, nudging her. She turned her head

around and stared at the TV.

"Your creation, Amanda. It got out of the bottle, like a genie. Maybe it will grant America three wishes."

"Bullshit, Alex."

"What other explanation could there be? Do you seriously believe the dude came back from the dead?"

"Of course not. But do you seriously believe that a virtual Lincoln that I programmed for another eccentric rich client somehow escaped from cyberspace and has invaded real space? That's just crazy."

"You know what I think. That there is no difference between reality and virtual reality."

"That's bullshit, Alex."

"So what do you think?"

"You know what I think. He's a Lincoln impersonator, that's all. The greatest ever. And the world's biggest con artist. Bigger than Donald Trump."

"A con artist who might get elected president."

"Aren't all presidents con artists? It's in the job description."

"What about the DNA match?"

"A trick. A con. Just like everything. Just like Dreamworlds, Alex. The Noble Lie."

"Listen." He nudged her again and turned up the volume on the TV. They both looked at it.

Abraham Lincoln had been cleaned up. His beard was neatly trimmed but he still looked cadaverous as he always had, cheeks deeply sunken. But his nappy hair had been nicely trimmed and combed and he wore a modern power suit and tie, with an American flag stickpin. The suit was powder-blue and the tie blood-red. His gray eyes as always danced with mischief and a devilish grin occasionally leavened his somber expression. He looked bemused as his interrogator interviewed him.

It was a new program on Fox News called POW! and the interviewer was a brash young journalist on the make.

"It's a honor to have you on POW!, Mr. Lincoln," said the interviewer, whose name was Trevor Credence. The boyish journo with the blow-dried hair wore a red bow tie and looked like the president of a collegiate Young Republicans club and a member of a racist fraternity, which is to say, a member of a fraternity. "Let's cut to the chase, sir. Are you running for president, or not?" Along the bottom of the screen a ticker of sports scores, celebrity sightings, the latest Muslim terrorist attacks and Wall Street earnings reports flowed, under the date: January 20, 2016. It had been nine months since Lincoln had risen from the dead, and the New Hampshire primary was just over the horizon. It was exactly one year until the successor to Barack Obama would be inaugurated.

Then a flash poll appeared where the ticker had been: "Lincoln's modern dress: Yes or No?" The No's were winning by a landslide.

Lincoln's gray eyes twinkled with levity and he offered a slight, close-mouthed grin. Nodding, he said, "I must admit, young man, that the taste of it is in my mouth a little."

Tweets exploded across the Twitterverse. Blogs were updated in real time. Message boards buzzed. Cyberspace was afire. Trolls crawled out from under their digital bridges to torment their earnest interlocutors online.

"You heard it here first, ladies and gentlemen," the blow-dried blowhard interviewing Lincoln said. He believed that this scoop had set him up for life. "The Great Emancipator may toss his stovepipe hat into the ring."

Credence was about to ask another question when Lincoln said: "I could be bounded in a nutshell, and count myself a king of infinite space, were it not that I have bad dreams."

"What — what dreams, sir? What does that mean?"

"Why, son, as I'm sure you're aware, they kept me in a madhouse for eight months after I returned to this mortal coil until they made a DNA match last month and proved that I am, who I am. Then they let me out. That unpleasant experience accounts for my bad dreams. I must say that since then I have studied up a bit on DNA and genetics. It's quite fascinating. Though I recall taking a look at that book by Darwin round 'bout 1860. I was amazed to discover that he was born on the same day and year that I was. At that time, after thumbing through Darwin's book, I told my law partner Herndon that such stuff was not for ordinary minds like mine."

"So you agree, sir, that evolution is nonsense?" A new flash poll was superimposed on the TV screen under the two men: "Evolution: True or False?" False was already winning with eighty percent.

"I agree that I have an ordinary mind, young man. Notwithstanding all the silly hagiography about me I see in the bookstores and on this amazing thing called the Internet. I'm just humble old Abe Lincoln, same as I ever was." Lincoln offered another close-mouthed, enigmatic smile.

"But, sir, what about Paradise 72 Inc., the radical Muslim terrorist multinational corporation that has bought much of the Middle East and claims to have robbed your grave and is holding your corpse hostage for billions of dollars?" A split-screen appeared, the talking Lincoln on the left and the alleged Lincoln corpse on the right, nailed to a cross in crucifixion pose and surrounded by hooded, black-clad jihadists pointing Kalashnikovs at the moldering beanstalk, stovepipe hate askance on a decayed face through which patches of skull showed, the face like a sinister Halloween-mask parody of Lincoln's real face.

"What about 'em, son?"

"But, Mr. Lincoln, some people claim that this corpse proves that you're a fraud, after all, notwithstanding the DNA match, which after all could have been faked. Also, no one likes or trusts scientists and their global warming fraud. No one likes or trusts anyone anymore. Anyway, what do you think of these Muslim terrorists with WASP business minds, and — should you be restored to high office — how do you plan on dealing with the existential threat that they pose to the American way of life?"

"In my day, son, we didn't have too much contact with Mooslims and Hindoos and suchlike. So I'd have to study up on the matter. I do recall having some interactions with the Injuns. One day a tribe visited me in the Oval Office and I explained to them that the world was a great big ball."

"Greatest con artist ever," Amanda Clocker said with plain admiration.

"Your creation."

"Bullshit."

"Is it?"

"Kill the volume," Clocker said. "I'm sick of this Lincoln shit."

"Wait."

"What?"

"Look."

A bloated, arm-waving, orange-faced and orange-haired pestilence now filled the screen. He appeared to be a cross between a human and an orangutan. He was like animate pus in human form squeezed into a red tie and a blue suit with an American flag lapel pin about as big and gaudy as a neon sign advertising a Las Vegas casino with a strip joint and a brothel in back. He was making grotesque faces and aping "Ape" Lincoln as he called the former president, drawing himself inward and upward and pretending to walk with Lincoln's clumsy, raw-boned gait. A mad mob was cheering wildly for him, red, white and blue signs jabbing up and down on sticks. MAKE AMERICA GREAT AGAIN, the signs screamed. The short-fingered vulgarian fluttered his little digits on his pudgy paws and roared, "I like presidents who *don't* get shot!"

"Bring back the Confederacy!" a confederacy of dunces roared in unison. "Bring back slavery"

Some black protesters protested.

"Rough them up!" The Donald roared. "They *deserve* to be roughed up!"

A mob descended.

"For the love of Christ, turn off the fucking TV," Clocker said. "I think I'm going to puke."

World turned it off.

Clocker sighed. "Escape. Even *I* want to escape now. Like Hickenlooper."

"How's he like it so far?"

"He *loves* it."

"He's had a tour?"

"I dropped him in Vegas in 1962. He gambled away a virtual fortune. Bitcoins."

"Why Vegas?"

"He wanted to see the Rat Pack. They were performing at some casino."

"Martinis, cigarettes, sexism, racism, homophobia and gambling," World said. "The Mad Men era. You know our Mr. Hickenlooper."

Still stretched out on top of him, she raised her head and looked him in the eye. "I want you to leave your wife,

Alex. To be with me all the time."

"I can't do that."

"Why not? You don't love her."

"I have a kid now. Just born. A son, an heir. I named him Alex Jr. I want for him to conquer the rest of the world that I didn't. I want him to conquer the real world."

"But everything is in the mind, according to you. To exist is to be perceived, remember? That's why, according to you, I can program a virtual Lincoln and he can escape from cyberspace like a genie from a bottle. But if you don't perceive him he fails to exist, right? Because to exist is to be perceived. *Esse est percipi*, remember?"

"What are you getting at, Amanda?"

"Your wife and kid only exist if you perceive them. Right now they don't exist. All you are perceiving is me. Therefore, I am all that there is."

She raked her hand through her long, wild hair, pushing it back over her head. With her slanted, catlike green eyes and a smile that seemed to consist of little ridged teeth, like that of a wild animal, she fairly growled at him, her voice a husky, urgent whisper: "Delete them, Alex. In the final analysis, they're just pixels in the pixie palace of your mind." World had told his wife that he was pulling an all-nighter at the office to continue the Hickenlooper project.

She reached for her pack of Marlboros on the table next to them, took out a cigarette and lighted it. She blew smoke toward the ceiling. He wrinkled his nose. "You even smoke after sex," he observed, though this had not been the first time that she had lighted up after they had lighted up each other. She said: "Do I smoke after sex? I never looked to see if I do."

"A techno-monarchy."

"What?"

"That's what America really needs. Not Lincoln. Not The Donald. Not even democracy. Democracy is a sham, the theory of a drunk looking for his lost keys under a street lamp because that's where the light is. A techno-monarchy would combine traditional, long-successful hierarchal modes of being with the technologically wisest at the top."

"The wisest being?"

"Techno-nerds. Like me. And like you, Amanda. King Alex and his Queen Amanda."

"This Dark Enlightenment shit of yours."

"Yes."

Amanda was silent, a contemplative look in her slanted eyes. She meditatively blew smoke rings.

"With you on top of civilization, Amanda. Just like you're on top in bed."

When he fell asleep in Amanda Clocker's arms, he dreamed of a black sun and white shadows. The world as a photographic negative. Then he dreamed that space was time, and the long white shadow of a rail-thin rail splitter in a stovepipe hat was cast across the continents of the centuries, the thunderous boot falls of the shadow's source reverberating across the pages of the ages like the footfalls of God.

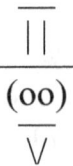

The self-styled Posse Comitatus, fueled by drink and demons and dreams and under the spur of impulse, left Whitely, Idaho, on April 15, 2015, in two pickup trucks, one of which belonged to Shit Free and the other to Boris the anarchist. Their numbers consisted of Boris, Shit Free or Die and his girlfriend The Bike, Red Dave, Milton the Libertarian and Roderick the Objectivist. Their initial plan was to drive straight to Washington, D.C., where they planned to overthrow the government by some unspecified means. Their journey began auspiciously enough. They managed to make it all the way to Wyoming, where they stopped at a roadhouse and got drunk while arguing politics. The central dispute was over the form of government that they would install in Washington to replace the toppled Obama regime. Clearly their political aims were incompatible. Vast quantities of Gutbuster beer were consumed, and it is believed that shots were both consumed and later fired. The local police were summoned, and the night was painted red with the revolving lights of squad cars. More shots were fired, possibly including an exchange of fire between the Posse and the police, but the whole episode is clouded in obscurity owing to the author's inebriation. The upshot is that the disputatious inebriates escaped into the night, but they pointed their pickups in the wrong direction and it was not until they were in Nevada that they discovered they were heading toward California and not the nation's capital. They fought over GPS software in the hope of correcting their trajectory, until the voice of the software that kept trying to recalculate their route fell indignantly silent. On the spur of the moment they decided to drive to San Francisco and overthrow its government first as a dress rehearsal for the seizure of the nation's capital.

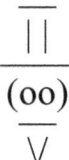

"I've signed a contract."

"Break it."

"He's paying me — us — a fortune."

"You've sold your soul to him."

"We're set up for life with this money."

"Break the contract, Elvis, before it breaks you."

Elvis Kandor, aka Cyrus Clone, also known as Cyclone, held a fork in one hand and a knife in the other, and stared down squeamishly at the plate of Alabama crawfish that he had ordered from room service. The crawfish resembled the burned-out husks of miniature land-crawling remote-controlled drones designed by a mad scientist at the Pentagon to spy on Americans. He and his spouse, John Caswell, were having dinner in their hotel suite. They were in a suburb of Mobile, Alabama, a bland expanse of cookie-cutter housing projects, soulless industrial parks and road signage importuning motorists to let Jesus into their hearts before it was too late. The window of their room looked out on a depressing used-car lot festooned with brightly colored red and blue pennants. A giant Confederate battle flag wafted overheard, affixed to a towering flagpole. Its shadow drifted menacingly over the macadam. It was the new national flag of the Second Confederacy, which included all the states of the Old Confederacy, except for Texas, which had set up on its own. The Rocky Mountain States were also part of the new nation. The date was February 9, 2016. The New Hampshire primary was underway for both parties. Eight days earlier, Lincoln had won the Iowa caucuses of both parties as a write-in candidate, which had provoked an explosive and mocking attack on Lincoln by G.O.P. candidate Donald Trump, who had led the polls before the caucuses. "I like presidents who *don't* look like apes!"

an embittered Trump, who looked like an orangutan, had tweeted on Twitter.

"A rally tomorrow in Mobile," Kandor muttered, looking with dubiety at the monsters on the plate, "and then a huge rally next week in Atlanta. They love me. You know that I always wanted to be an actor. For the movies. I never realized that dream, but maybe I got not what I wanted, but what I needed."

Caswell leaned forward across the table and looked fiercely at his husband.

"You're saying you *enjoy* doing what you're doing? Pretending to be something you're not? A radical, fire-breathing right-wing bigot? A man agitating for the final breakup of the Union?"

"Yes, John. I *do* enjoy it. I thought that the best that I could do was acting on Web video. Virtual acting. But it turns out I can turn on a crowd in person. They believe in me. They believe in me, even though they know I'm a fraud. It's common knowledge that we're married and I'm a political liberal. But the hicks down here, the rubes and rebels all across the New Confederacy, they come out to see me at my rallies and they roar their approval as I call for the new government in Richmond to hold its ground. Which is easy to do. Obama still can't make up his mind whether to use force or not to put down the rebellion. Do you know what I'm going to say in Atlanta? I'm going to call for the resurrection of slavery, and for the reinstitution of sodomy laws against faggots like us ... Oh, don't look so shocked! Do you have any idea what a high it is to turn on a crowd? It's better than sex. Speaking of which, I'm also calling for the government in Richmond to ban abortion and birth control, and to repeal women's suffrage."

Kandor teased up a dead crawfish with the tines of his fork and bit into it tentatively. It crunched between his teeth, the sound of metal imploding during a terrorist attack, possibly as the result of an improvised explosive device detonating. He chewed with difficulty, swallowed laboriously and then set down his fork. He patted his napkin to his lips and then set it down and looked at Caswell.

Caswell looked at him.

Kandor rose from the table, wandered over to the liquor cabinet and poured himself a drink. He said: "And the best part of it is, Hickenlooper is paying me to do something I love to do. Paying me a fortune. To do something I love so much, I'd do it for free if I could afford to do so. Honestly, if he weren't so old and disgusting, I think I might suck his crooked cock. He must be a fag, even though fags like us disgust him. He never got married, after all. A self-hating closet case."

Caswell slammed both fists down on the dinner table, and shot to his feet. He strode over and grabbed his husband by the shoulders, and then whirled him around until the two men were face to face. Caswell shook Kandor and roared at him: "This is becoming more than make believe. You're becoming the very thing that you hate."

Kandor shrugged out of Caswell's grasp and strode across the room. He lifted the drink to his lips. He had been drinking lavishly lately, raiding the liquor cabinets of hotel suites across the South. Suites subsidized by Homer Hickenlooper, who had bought Kandor's soul. At least it hadn't come cheap, Kandor consoled himself. But come it had.

Disgusted, Caswell grabbed the remote and turned on the TV in the suite. He surfed through some cable stations until he found a news channel. Exit polls in New Hampshire predicted that Abraham Lincoln would win both the Republican and Democratic primaries on write-in votes. The resurrected president had not yet thrown his stovepipe hat into the ring or even said much at all about public policy matters, preferring instead, for inscrutable reasons of his own, to maintain a cagey silence. The bloated orange-haired monster was a close second in the Republican New Hampshire race, however, and was tweeting that the election had been stolen and making vague allusions to violence to set the results right.

"Jesus Christ," Caswell muttered, watching the exit poll results flashed on the screen. "Is the world mad? What do you think of this character impersonating Lincoln? He may sweep into the Oval Office by acclamation."

"He's a false-flag operation."

"Excuse me?"

"A government project. He may not even be real, just a robot or an android, or a virtual reality projection. The government invented Lincoln to intimidate the New Confederacy back into the Union by throwing the specter of its greatest nemesis at them. But the New South will not be intimidated by this fakery."

Caswell studied his husband, who had just parroted the rantings on the memescape of the right-wing blogosphere and Twitterverse, the fulminations of the wingnuts that began as soon as Lincoln was released from the madhouse when it was determined that his DNA was a match for the long-dead, but now newly alive, 16th president. As far as science could tell, this was the real Lincoln.

"So you agree with the crazies?" Caswell asked.

"Well what do *you* think, John? Do you really think he is Lincoln come back to life? That's the craziest idea of all. It's amusing to see the scientists on the side of the resurrection. Mixing religion with science, indeed! Of course he's an impersonator, as you yourself just said. But this time the so-called crazies, as you call them, have got it right. It is a false-flag operation, just like 9/11, the Boston Marathon bombing, Benghazi, and many other so-called acts of terror."

"You're acting now, right, Elvis? Please tell me that you're acting. All the world's a stage and all that? Because your act is itself an act of terror. To me, anyway."

"Or maybe he really is old Abe Lincoln. In that case, he's the real Lincoln posing as a Lincoln impersonator impersonating the real Lincoln. The world's stage is strange, John. A strange stage. I've found that out since my association with Homer Hickenlooper began. It's a labyrinth of conspiracies, a terrifying rat's maze of black book operations, black helicopters, Men in Black and a black president born blackly in Kenya. We've got Manchurian candidates all around us. Beware, John. The government is coming to take away our guns and plant computer chips in our brains so they can control us remotely from Washington and propagandize us with Godless materialist secularism. That's what Homer said. I believe it. I surely do."

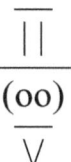

The Gang arrived in San Francisco a couple of days after their drunken shootout with the cops in Wyoming. They found the city to be surprisingly congenial despite its advancing colonization and gentrification by code-writing dot-com crud, and put off their plans to overthrow it as a dress rehearsal for overthrowing the government. Red Dave joined a Marxist collective in the Mission District, where he wrote articles on Socialism for its Web site. Milton took a job with a Libertarian think tank. Roderick the Objectivist found like-minded Ayn Randroids and they began pooling their resources with the ultimate objective of buying some property in rural Humboldt County to set up a Galt's Gulch there, where they would support themselves by growing and selling marijuana. Boris the Anarchist took a job as a clerk at City Lights bookstore and met its owner, Lawrence Ferlinghetti, still alive and even spry at age 97. Shit Free got involved in selling drugs and a motorcycle gang and pimped The Bike in the seedy Tenderloin district to make some extra cash. He also found work as a guitar player in a Christian Nazi rock band called Holycaust, which gave a great vibe in the rollicking Soma nightclubs. The Gang stayed in touch via e-mail with Sam the bartender back in Whitely, who always replied typically cryptically. Luckily the Gang found a nice flat to share in pricey Pacific Heights, paid for by Roderick, who reasoned that he was not being altruistic but acting in his own self-interest, for he clung irrationally to the delusion that someday he would convert all his friends to Objectivism. The building was owned by Homer Hickenlooper, who frequently visited it as he obsessively and possessively did all his properties, his properties being synonymous with his identity: I own, therefore I am.

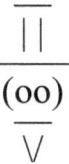

By early March, both the Democrats and Republicans, alarmed by the Lincoln write-in bubble, had banned write-in votes. Lincoln had still not declared his intentions. Yet a riven nation turned its lonely eyes to him, a black-clad specter in a stovepipe hat who had stepped out of the pages of antebellum America and set his dusty boots squarely down in the sleek cybernetic 21st century. But with Lincoln write-in votes debarred, the Orange-Haired Monster swept the Super Tuesday primaries and then bragged about his dick size. He also mercilessly mocked Abraham Lincoln, as well as Jesus and God ("I like saviors who *aren't* crucified!") When he did, his poll numbers soared. It seemed it would be a two-man showdown between Abraham Lincoln and The Donald, if only the resurrected president would take the plunge and throw his stovepipe hat into the ring: a ring more like a World Wrestling Federation ring than anything else. Sober pundits muttered that America was not just breaking up, but going insane. Then the sober pundits got drunk to drown their sorrows.

The nation was divided in a more fundamental way: On one side were the realists, who maintained that this Lincoln really was Lincoln; and on the other side was a smaller (but growing) faction called the Corpsists, who felt that this "Lincoln" was a fraud and that the real Lincoln was the corpse, crucified and under further threat of beheading, that was being held hostage by the multinational Muslim jihadists. P72 had aimed a Webcam at the crucified corpse and broadcast on the Web video of it 24/7 for a sign-in fee. They were making millions. Unless the U.S. paid up, the jihadists warned, they would behead the corpse and then cremate the head and body and "scatter the ashes in the Holy Land of the Levant, so that the footsteps of the faithful, the followers of the Prophet Muhammad (PBUH) and of ALLAH (PBUH), may trod upon that ashen corruption and grind it underfoot. Inshallah."

Lincoln lived with Officer Sully Stark and Stark's wife Hortense, who was slipping every further into the darkness of Alzheimer disease. The Haitian nurse who cared for Hortense and who also lived with them performed her grim chores in solemn silence. There had been some talk of amending the law to let Lincoln occupy his old Springfield home, which was a national historic site managed by the National Park Service, but the 16th president demurred, stating that he could not imagine living "in that drafty old barn" without his beloved Molly, who remained dead and gone. Stark, who had taken early retirement, served as Lincoln's personal bodyguard, though a retinue of local cops, among them Sully's old partner, Ron Boyle (high-strung and bifurcated as ever, believing in the white of Good and the black of Evil with no shades of gray between) had been assigned to guard the Stark/Lincoln household 24/7. Stark, leery of his former partner, had resolved through back channels to quietly veto Boyle's presence in the attachment, but hearing of his idea, Lincoln had waved Stark off, saying, "I see something in that boy Boyle. I surely do."

"What?" a surprised Stark had asked.

But Lincoln would not say, lapsing into an abstracted silence, his gray and unfocused eyes seemingly fixed on some enigmatic inner vision that he chose not to share. He had looked particularly melancholy at that moment.

The cops were charged to ward off the inevitable pilgrimages of gawkers and grifters, autograph seekers, political opportunists, con artists, fast-buck abracadabra charlatans, news media goons, loners and losers seeing an answer — an epiphany of some sort — and a surprising number of Evangelical Christians from the newly rebellious South who in Lincoln's Second Coming perceived a parallel with Jesus, just as his long-ago assassination on Good Friday had been redolent with religious overtones. A consensus seemed to be coalescing around that idea that Lincoln reincarnate could not only prevent the division of the country by the sheer force of his mythic presence, but that he might be able to solve all other problems in the world as well. The notion of an actual savior, a man on horseback, was anathema to both major political parties, which is why they had quelled the write-in campaigns: if someone actually *could* solve all problems, they realized, then both parties would be put out of business. All the while Lincoln maintained a mostly Sphinx-like silence, rationing his comments on his newly acquired Twitter account. He was "studying up on history and current events," he tweeted once, and another time he allowed as how "the world is greatly more complex and, in a sense, utterly stupefying, compared with the much simpler world of my original time." And then silence, even though he had used only 129 of his allotted 140 characters. Moving through the courts was the question of whether a dead man come back to life who had already been elected president twice a century and a half ago was even eligible to run again, should he choose. The issue was ultimately decided by the Supreme Court, which ruled in Lincoln's favor by a vote of 5-4, with Chief Justice John Roberts surprisingly providing the swing vote against the court's conservatives, who preferred that Lincoln drop dead again.

One day Stark had left the house to run some errands. The nurse had a rare few days off and was away to tend to unspecified personal matters. Lincoln had promised to watch over Hortense, who was usually manageable in the middle of the day, generally napping for several hours.

"It's not a bother, Sully," Lincoln had assured his friend, who had protested, not wanting to put Lincoln out. "Run your errands. Take your time."

Stark returned home, slipped the key into the front door lock and entered the house, a bag of groceries under one arm. He stopped when he heard voices coming his wife's bedroom: "Now, Molly," Lincoln was saying.

"Now, Molly. It's all right."

Confused, Stark started toward the bedroom but stopped and listened for a few moments. He then detoured into the kitchen, where he deposited the bag of groceries on a countertop. Then he walked softly back toward the bedroom, the voices becoming more audible as he approached.

He stopped at the threshold of the open door and then looked around it and peered into the bedroom, not announcing his presence.

Hortense sat on the edge of the bed, in her night clothes. Her uncombed gray hair frazzled electrically outward around her head, and her eyes were the usual blank silver coins. Her mouth was ajar, a long string of yellow drool hanging down from one corner of it. Her slippered feet were composed upon the floor and Lincoln was lankly bent, perched on one knee. With a wet rag he was cleaning up something on the floor. Then the stench, and the truth, hit Stark, and his nostrils contracted in disgust mingled with despair.

"I am Mrs. President Abraham Lincoln," Stark's wife babbled, beginning to rock back and forth on the bed. "I am Mrs. President Abraham Lincoln."

"There, there, Molly," Lincoln said in a gentling, amiable tone of voice as he cleaned up the demented woman's bowel slops. "You just relax, and we'll have everything cleaned up in no time."

Stark watched, agog, not daring to reveal himself, as Lincoln cleaned while consoling Hortense, who suddenly had decided that she was Mary Todd Lincoln.

Is it I who is insane? flashed through the retired sergeant's mind.

"Willie!" Hortense suddenly shrieked. "Where's our Willie? Where is he, Mr. President Lincoln?"

"A better place, Molly." He had gathered up a big handful of the wet rags that he had used to clean the floor and was rising stiffly to his feet when he glanced at the door and saw Stark peering into the room from around the door frame.

"Oh, hello there, Sully," Lincoln sang out in jovial greeting, as if nothing untoward were going on. "Molly — I mean Hortense — just had a little accident. Nothing to be alarmed about."

Stark felt tears start to his eyes, and he choked up.

"You ... you didn't have to do that ... Mr. President. It could have ... waited till I got back." He brought the back of his hand to his eyes to wipe away tears, and when he did he felt Lincoln's large hand on his round shoulder.

"Not a bother at all," Lincoln said, the befouled rags in his other hand. "Accidents happen from time to time. It needed to be tended to at once. You'd best run her a bath."

Later, the two men discussed what had happened over cups of coffee in the kitchen. Hortense had been bathed and put back to bed.

"I apologize," Lincoln said in a tender voice.

Stark had raised the coffee cup to his lips, and now over the rim of the cup with his sad, bloodshot eyes, he regarded Lincoln with surprise.

"Apologize? For what?" He lowered the cup to the saucer.

"I'm afraid my presence here isn't doing her much good," Lincoln said in voice tinged with melancholy. "She thinks she's Molly Lincoln, now. She thinks she's my wife, not yours."

Stark closed his hands around the cup and gazed moodily down into the coffee, a curl of steam rising from it.

"An icon of world history kneeling as though in

prayer before my mindless wife, cleaning up her shit," Stark observed bluntly. "And you, apologize to me? You didn't have to do that. But you did."

Lincoln began to speak but Stark cut him off: "She doesn't know me anymore, or even herself. It doesn't matter if she thinks she's your wife. If you hadn't been here, she would have thought that she was someone else's wife. Anyone but *my* wife. I've lost her, Lincoln. For good."

Lincoln leaned forward and patted Stark's knee. Apparently, though, he could find nothing to say. With shaking hands, Stark lifted the cup back to his lips, took a sip, and then set it down again. He wiped tears from his eyes.

"Willie … your son Willie ..." Stark was trying to remember history.

"He died while Molly and I were in the White House," Lincoln said. "It nearly killed my wife. She was never the same after."

"And your wife?"

"As I have subsequently learned after returning to this sad mortal coil, she died alone in an insane asylum years after my assassination. And not only that, my son Taddy, whom we adored, also died a few years after my assassination. He was only seventeen. Then of course our first son, Eddy, died in childbirth. Only Robert made it to adulthood and lived a long, full life, thank God."

Stark watched Lincoln's face, that sad, tawny, weatherbeaten expanse of leathery flesh. Stark believed that he had never seen a man look so sad. There was a long silence. Then Lincoln said: "Kneeling down to clean up some helpless person's shit counts every bit as much as ending slavery and winning the Civil War."

"You believe that?"

"I do. Kindness is all that counts. All that there is. Everything else is illusion, or delusion. No one needs a president, a preacher, or anyone else to change the world. Change yourself. That's how to change the world." After a thoughtful pause, he added: "I didn't free the slaves. Not really. They freed themselves."

Lincoln lapsed again into moody silence, and then abruptly returned to the topic of his son Robert.

"The hell of it is," Lincoln said, his head tilted to one side and slowly moving up and down, "Robert and I never much even liked each other. He was a great disappointment to me, and, I suppose, I to him."

"Kevin."

Lincoln looked askance at Stark, with an expression of melancholy curiosity. Stark had been vague, even evasive, on the topic of his only child, whom he had personally arrested when Kevin was fourteen. Now Kevin was doing ten to twenty at Big Muddy for armed robbery.

Stark confessed this all to Lincoln for the first time.

Lincoln absorbed the story with a stoic, impartial expression, now and then nodding solemnly as Stark made his points. When Stark had finished after a silence that stretched to a painful length, Lincoln gazed off into middle distance, inclined his great haggard head and said with utmost feeling: "When I knelt before your wife today, I felt that I was kneeling before all of suffering humanity."

A solemn silence. Only the ticking of a clock could be heard. The cup of coffee was back at Stark's lips. He drained the dregs of it. Lincoln broke the silence in an offhand way: "Sully, how'd you like to be vice president of the United States?"

The coffee shot out of Stark's mouth.

"Or even president, should it come to that."

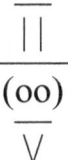

At the same time in Seattle, Alexander World, alone in his Dreamworlds office in Seattle, his back to the big plate-glass window that offered a sweeping view of downtown, was thinking that April was the cruelest month. It had rained for fifteen straight days, and behind him the window wept bitter tears. Seattle was barely visible in the miasma of grayish rain and ghoulish fog that had settled over the city like a graveyard curse. World had not seen the sun in fifteen days, and he began to fear that he would never see it again.

He drummed his fingers on the top of his desk and stared vacantly at the blank screen of his laptop, which he had turned off. He had ordered his secretary to debar all visitors and communications from the outside world.

World had been all over the world since bursting on the scene a little more than two years ago with his quantum computation breakthrough that had made possible DreamGlass for the hoi polloi and complex, detail-rich alternative universes for the filthy rich like Homer Hickenlooper. In so doing he had made himself filthy rich, which meant that he could afford to build his own Dreamworld and escape into it, perhaps forever. A way out other than suicide, which he had first contemplated at age five. What had kept him going during the long lonely years of exile, of feeling that he did not belong among other people, was his brilliance at computer programming, a brilliance that rendered him an outcast in high school and a misfit in early adulthood until he caught lightning in a bottle by overturning Heisenberg's Uncertainty Principle and making quantum computation scalable and affordable.

He had a wife, a kid — three months old, his heir — but he also had a mistress. He was living a double life. He was sitting on a pile of money. And he felt responsible for the return of Abraham Lincoln, with whatever unpredictable consequences that the president's resurrection betokened or perhaps even entailed. The jury was out on that one. The nation, meanwhile, was suspended in limbo as the presidential campaign unfolded, the New Confederacy a de facto going concern while President Obama dithered over what to do about the second secession.

But it seemed, in truth, that everyone in America, perhaps even the world, was waiting for word from the sixteenth president of the United States, who was holed up in Springfield while the world held its breath, and who was, so he tweeted, "studying up on the situation."

The sky darkened yet more and the rain hammered down on the plate-glass window. World became so morose that he lacked the energy to keep his head up. His face fell into his forearms crossed upon the desk. He sighed. The rain rattled piteously on the pane. It will rain tonight, too, he thought, and tomorrow. It will come down tomorrow and tomorrow and tomorrow, all our tomorrows until the final tomorrow when life is rounded by a little sleep. It will come down. Let it come down.

He suddenly repented everything that he had created. DreamGlass was transforming the hoi polloi, especially teenagers, into idiots immersed in brainless video games that seemed as real as reality, but more inviting. The ultimate escape, a techno-drug that made LSD look like pabulum. As for Dreamworlds, those rich and immersive alternative histories like the one that Amanda Clocker had so brilliantly programmed for Hickenlooper, they disgusted him. What good were they? Of what possible use were they to humanity at large? Did they feed anyone? No. Did they give anyone housing, jobs, dignity? No, no and no.

Then he remembered that he was Darkly Enlightened. Or he supposed that he was, at any rate. He now wondered: Had Hickenlooper planted a little poison in his mind, during their first meeting?

With his face still buried in his folded arms he remembered, with a spasm of guilt, that he did not have much use for humanity. Then he supposed, or hoped, that while he had no use for humanity as a whole, he thought highly of individual people, who had always tormented him while he was growing up. Or maybe it was the other way around? That he cared not for individuals, but for humanity in the abstract? Which was it? Which was it *supposed* to be? Did it matter anymore? Was he darkly enlightened or lightly endarkened?

He remembered visiting New York City for a conference about a year and a half ago, and how the city had presented itself as a George Grosz drawing. The commuters packed into the subway trains for the rush-hour commute became, in his mind's eye, Jews packed onto trains en route to the Dachaus of their dead-end jobs, their drab and meaningless lives. The face of an ordinary hot-dog stand vendor had taken on the sinister aspect of a gargoyle, his coat transformed into bat wings and his pupils red dots in yellow balls. A dog, a little toy poodle, had trotted up to him on the sidewalk. He had tried to pet it. Suddenly its ears inflated to grotesque proportions, and its tongue fell out of its maw and slithered across the pavement like a snake. Its teeth were daggers, and its eyes were orange, like Donald Trump's neon-bright hair. BllllLLLAAAARGH! the dog roared, and fire shot out of its mouth, singing his pants. *The Pood*, he thought. *This dog is called The Pood.* He had to cut short his visit and fly back to Seattle, hyperventilating periodically during the flight. Panic attacks, depression. A nightmare of a trap door opening under his feet and he falling, falling, falling forever into that bottomless and awful oubliette. Voices in his head.

"Surprise!"

It was a voice in his head.

He realized that he had fallen half asleep, and now with effort he raised his head and rubbed the sleep from his eyes. When he was sitting up again, Amanda Clocker sat across from his at his desk, her gorgeous gams crossed provocatively. Short, short skirt. She was smiling beguilingly at him and holding something in her outstretched hands that he did not recognize. Then he did.

"Your own Dreamworld," she said, holding the wraparound shades out toward him. "I programmed it for you. As a gift. Happy birthday! Put them on."

"It's my birthday?"

"Yes."

What card was she playing now? Their love affair was increasingly hard to conceal. She continued to press him to leave his wife and kid and shack up with her: "Delete them," she said. Delete them, like pixels on a computer screen. DELETE. DELETE. DELETE. Drag to trash and empty the trash. Down, down the rat holes of cyberspace. Down and done. Gone.

"Put them on," she said, an edge to her voice. Her palms angled out over his desk and the wraparounds that she held were now right under his nose, gold rims and black lenses. Like two giant bees waiting to sting him.

"I asked my secretary not to let any visitors in."

"I told him you had summoned me, and he believed it. Put them on, Alex."

He put them on.

He was home with his wife and his heir.

Except they were figures out of a George Grosz drawing.

Ecce Homo.

His wife was a hooker.

His three-month-old son, Alex Jr., was a demon child. From its crib, it looked up at him with a gimlet eye and then smiled, showing a single fang grown from the left side of its mouth. Its right eye was closed, but its left eye, with which it had skewered World, gradually swelled up to immense proportions, as large as a white cue ball with the pupil painted on it. World screamed.

His wife, Cassie, dressed in slut's finery, was butchering a pig with a meat cleaver. Blood flowed, dark red. He grabbed the meat cleaver from her and cut her throat. DELETE. Then he butchered the demon child, and DELETED him, too. He carried their remains to a trash bucket, and threw their corpses in. The bodies, too big to be accommodated by the container, hung heavy-limbed over the rim of it, but he went to his laptop and clicked his cursor on DELETE TRASH and then the bodies were gone, the wastebasket emptied. He took off the wraparounds and threw them clattering across the desktop. Amanda Clocker watched him with a catlike grin, the ridges of her teeth showing like those of a family pet gone feral.

"You're fired," he said.

"Am I?"

"Get out."

"You deleted them, didn't you, Alex? Now your eyes are on me. All eyes are on me."

He grabbed for his cellphone to call Cassie. But she stayed his hand with hers.

"Of course they are still alive," she said in a

patronizing tone of voice, suggesting that she was addressing an idiot. "I was just proving to you that there is a difference between real reality and virtual reality. When you get home, your loving housewife and your slumbering heir, that little blob of protoplasm that bears your genes, will be waiting for you as always in your lovely home. But, Alex, you'll never see them in the same way again, after what you just saw. Will you?"

He bolted out of the office. Amanda Clocker smiled with delight. She believed herself to be the most powerful person on earth. With her programming skills, she was in possession of the fire of Prometheus. She had given fire to Man. She did not care about the rest of the legend, only the fire. She now turned her attention to tweaking Hickenlooper's Dreamworld. He had wanted Goldwater elected in 1964. Done. But she thought it might be amusing for President Goldwater to unleash a nuclear war while Hickenlooper was inside his Dreamworld. Say, in August 1965. The whole world up in flames!

Done.

She smiled, and threw back her hair. She stretched, and laughed. Her teeth glittered with malice.

When he got home, Alexander World felt as if he were moving through heavy liquid, like congealing glass. It warped the dim rainy light and gave everything a circus funhouse aspect, the world seen through distorting mirrors. His limbs were heavy, and he felt himself treading upstream and fighting for breath. The relentless rain beat on the windowpanes like buckshot on a tin roof. Lighting forked the sky, illuminating the interior of the house with a blue-white wash that momentarily banished all shadows, and then a deafening crack of thunder shook the house as in an earthquake. The rumbling that followed sounded like the groaning of a wounded animal. He was soaked, drooling water as he ripped off his wraps and let them fall to the floor in the expanding puddle that he had made.

"Honey? The weather is terrible! You must be soaked." It was Cassie, calling from the kitchen. Odors of dinner cooking.

World looked at the furniture in the living room as if they were strangers at a dinner party whom he wished to avoid. The water sluiced off of him. His hair was a lank mat. Water dripped from the tip of his nose as from a leaky faucet.

He shuffled toward the kitchen. Another blinding fork of lightning split the sky, visible in the picture window, and it was followed by another deafening crack. The afterimage of the lightning burned on his retinas, and his ears rang. After the rumble of thunder faded, the windowpanes shuddered as the wind and rain lashed against them. The wind moaned, like Amanda in heat.

Cassie had been the only woman with whom World had slept until Amanda Clocker had seduced or blackmailed him into bed. When he met Cassie she was working as a barista at a trademark Seattle Starbucks — the *original* Starbucks, as a matter of fact, at Pike Place. She was not beautiful but she was not bad looking either. She was of average looks, and of average intelligence. Average. They had dated for about a year and she idolized him. He had asked her to marry him not because he loved her, but because he dimly perceived that he needed a wife. And an heir.

She idolized him so much that she did not question his endless late nights at the office. He doubted that she suspected anything. He doubted that she was able to be suspicious about him. She came out of the kitchen.

"Look at you," she fussed, smoothing his soaked hair with her hands. She kissed him on the lips and told him to get out of those wet clothes. Take a hot shower, for gosh sake! The thunder grumbled, and from another room came the sudden squalling of Alex Junior, three months old. He had been napping but now had been awakened by the storm, and Cassie hurried to his room to soothe him. World walked into the kitchen and saw a slaughtered pig lying on the floor in a pool of blood. Cassie had buried a hatchet in its side. The pig's gimlet eyes were wide open, and it looked up at him in blank bestial appraisal. Astounded, the entrepreneur yanked the hatchet from its hide and more blood squirted out of the pig's corpse. On the HTML chart the blood was hexadecimal red, #FF0000. He peered down at the pig, and it became a vague pink and red ensemble of pixels. Then it was gone, but the blood remained as did the hatchet in his hand, its blade dripping more blood onto the linoleum floor.

Another fork of lighting filled the house with a blue-white wash of light, and his infant son's voice rose into a ululating scream. World closed his hands behind his back with the hatchet in one of them and plodded into his son's room. Cassie's back was turned to him. She was holding their son, patting his back and soothing him. There, there. His chin rested on her shoulder and he could see his heir's face. Wrinkled and misshapen, it reminded him of a shrunken head prepared by a headhunter. The infant's eyes had been closed but now one of them opened, and father and son looked at each other across a gulf. Another flash of lightning lit up the room and when it did, his heir's open eye inflated like a balloon. The pupil seemed to have been painted on it. His heir grinned malevolently at him, and a fang gleamed. World staggered backward and then quietly slipped out of the room. The rain ticked on the roof. When Cassie had put their soothed son back in his crib, she came out of the room. He swung the hatchet at her. The blade hummed and he buried it in the center of her throat. It made a muffled *whomp* noise, like that of someone punching a pillow. Then it slicked through her spinal cord, which exploded in splinters, and continued out the back of her neck. A gout of blood geysered upward and her head floated toward the ceiling seemingly in slow motion, like a balloon released by a child. Then it abruptly fell to the floor with a thud and nestled up against the toes of his shoes like a bowling ball rolled down from a dispenser. Her two astounded eyes were located where the ball's finger holes should be. Her hair was uncharacteristically askew and her mouth ajar. Rivulets of blood leaked down from the corners of it and pooled on the floor.

"Delete," World muttered. He plodded back into his son's room with his back hunched Quasimodo-like, his arms crossed behind his back at the wrists with the hatchet dangling from his left hand. It dripped Cassie's blood.

When he reached the crib another blinding flash of lightning cast his long shadow against the far wall, raising the hatchet high over his head. The boom of thunder coincided with the thump of the blade. His little boy's head shot upward like a popped champagne cork, hit the ceiling and then fell to the floor. Outside a tree branch lashed furiously in gale-force winds. It broke through the window and whiplashed around the room amid a spray of glass fragments and needle-like rain. World threw up an arm to shield his eyes, and some of the shards cut his flesh. He regretted the loss of the window. A knothole in the tree's trunk regarded him balefully, like the eye of an Ent.

Afterward, in the kitchen, he dumped the remains of his wife and their heir into an oversized wastebasket, which was lined with a sturdy 39-gallon three-ply Glad plastic trash bag. Fortunately, the storm had abated; the lightning and thunder had made him jumpy, as if he had

had too much of Cassie's Starbucks coffee, which he had never particularly cared for anyway. He preferred Dunkin' Donuts coffee. He wandered into his den and sat down before his computer. With his cursor, he transferred the files of his dead wife and heir to the wastebasket icon on the desktop. He right-clicked and chose EMPTY TRASH. A message popped up: *Are you sure you want to empty the contents of this folder? They will be permanently deleted. Are you sure?*

He was sure.

With a cursor click the illusion of his wife and heir, those poor pixels, were swallowed up in a virtual black hole in some cynosure of cyberspace.

"Cassie, I'm home!" he sang out, feeling refreshed. He could smell dinner cooking in the kitchen. Red meat. He briskly rubbed his blood-soaked hands together. He had worked up an appetite.

Cassie?

Puzzled at receiving no response, he left his room and walked toward the kitchen. He was disquieted to see red fluid on the floor at the entrance to it: a broken bottle of Heinz ketchup, maybe.

"Honey? You broke the ketchup!"

When he entered the kitchen, he discovered that the floor was soaked with ketchup. Their bodies were still there, not deleted. They clogged the wastebasket like rebellious garbage, their lifeless limbs stretched out ungainly over the rim of it. Only their heads were missing. He had set them on a shelf in his den, to serve as slack-jawed and goggle-eyed bookends for his beloved computer manuals.

$$\frac{\overline{||}}{\underset{\overline{V}}{(oo)}}$$

On April 15, 2016, one year after rising from the dead and one hundred and fifty one years after dying, Abraham Lincoln tweeted the following message on his Twitter account:

Abe Lincoln @alincoln

I shall again seek the #presidency. Details to follow in a speech.

A mere sixty-six characters, with a hashtag. But the president had always been known for the brevity and concision of his utterances, his famed Gettysburg Address the speechifying 19th century equivalent of a modern Twitter oration. In fact, with some bemusement, Lincoln had recently told Sully and Hortense that he was going to try to tweet that address in 140 characters. Just for the hell of it.

That night, hours after Lincoln's terse tweet had lighted up cyberspace and thrown the mass media and social media into convulsions, Alexander World finally decided what to do about the wife and heir that he had dragged to the trash. For days he had tried to empty their trash on his computer, but never succeeded. It astonished him. The rain had stopped after a Noah-like forty days of downpour. End of the world. Or his world. He decided that he had to do something, because the corpses were rotting and stinking up the house.

Because he lived in the boonies, thirty miles outside Seattle, the nearest neighbors were about a mile away. That meant he could bury the bodies on his property with little risk of being spotted. So he did, that night. Still, it unnerved him that the skies had completely cleared, and a full moon shone down like a prison searchlight as he labored. Anyone who happened to be around would have seen his silhouette against the giant horizon-hugging moon, the shovel digging at the earth. The bodies going in. Then the shovel patting clods of dirt over them.

He had saved their heads as bookends. He contemplated them, and then he recalled that next Wednesday was Amanda Clocker's birthday. She had gifted him for his birthday. He owed her.

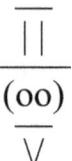

Two days after declaring for the presidency, Lincoln posted the following on his Twitter account:

Abraham Lincoln @alincoln

4 score 7 years ago, nu nation, all equal. Civil War. Many dead. Consecrate. Nu birth freedom. Nation of by 4 people not deleted from earth.

Success! One hundred and forty characters on the dot. Lincoln and Sully Stark had a rollicking laugh over it. "I declare," the president told his personal bodyguard and friend, with whom he liked to frequent the race track, "these tweets do make you get straight to the point, don't they? I reckon the blowhard politicians of my time would have been mortified by this technology. Hell, most of 'em were freaked out by the telegraph, which I loved. It was the Internet of my time."

Suddenly the smile ran from Lincoln's face. The change was as abrupt as a light switch turned from On to Off. Stark was chilled to see the laughter flash out and the grim gloom that suddenly veiled the president's homely features. Lincoln said somberly: "It will, however, be quite different when I address the public for the first time on the occasion of my declaring formally for the nation's highest office. I'm afraid, my dear Sully, that America's problems cannot be solved in a Twitter tweet." He clapped the ex-cop on the shoulder and said with even graver gravity leavened with a grim grin, "Now, son, which steed do you reckon most likely to win at Aqueduct tomorrow? Myself, I fancy that pale horse in the sixth race named Death."

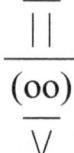

"I'm going to bankroll his campaign."

"But ... but *why*, in heaven's name?"

Homer Hickenlooper and Elvis Kandor, aka Cyclone, were meeting in Hickenlooper's San Francisco office.

"Because to run for president, one needs money, in this day and age, and lots of it. Even old Abe Lincoln."

"That's not my question," Cyclone said. "My question is, why do you want to bankroll his campaign? Do you know, unexpectedly, that a movement is sweeping the New Confederacy to vote for him? To annul secession? It's the Evangelical Christians. They think his resurrection puts him on par with Jesus, and is a clear sign from God that God wants the Union to remain intact. He could undo all our work, you and me, to split the Union, each for his own reason."

Homer Hickenlooper smiled bemusedly. Sometimes the few remaining strands of white hair atop his otherwise bald pate were curled into the shape of question marks. Other times, they boinged upward into exclamation points. Now they resembled quote marks. And quote he did. "'When you strike a king, you must kill him.' Emerson said that."

"What are you driving at?"

"Obviously this man is not really Abraham Lincoln, regardless of the DNA match story. Even the scientists who say his DNA proves he is Lincoln cannot accept the fact that a man has risen from the dead. It destroys their atheistic materialist world view. Somehow, somewhere, someone is playing a trick on all of us. I've told you about the false flag, the black box budgets and the Men in Black. This man is playing a trick on all of us. He's the joker in the deck. So we shall remove the joker. And when he's dead, he'll stay dead."

Cyclone was silent with incredulity. Hickenlooper said: "I'm going to bankroll his campaign because I want him to win as many votes as possible, and even for Lincoln, winning votes will take cash. Then, when candidate Lincoln is assassinated, as he shall be, that will be the final nail in the coffin of the Union. The Evangelicals will take it as a sign that God wants the South to rise again after all. And when this new Man on Horseback, this knight in shining armor, is put back into the earth, the demoralization of the public will be complete. And our goal shall be reached without any possibility of annulment."

"What in hell do you mean, *when* he is assassinated? You think someone is going to take a shot at him? Isn't that wishful thinking?"

"Not at all. I'm going to pay someone to kill him. Hire an assassin."

"Who?"

"You."

Kandor was dumbfounded.

"Well, you're an actor, Mr. Kandor — or should I say, Cyclone? You ought to be damned grateful to me, you fag. Not only did I pay you a bundle to take your schtick on the road, but I proved to you that you really *are* an actor, despite your previous youthful failures in the field.

You play the rubes like a violin. You think you sold your soul to me, sir, for thirty pieces of silver. As a matter of fact, I gave you your own soul back to you. I made you realize your potential." Hickenlooper leaned across the table, chortled, and patted the perplexed Cyclone on the shoulder. "Look here boy, you're an actor. Really."

"So?"

"And who killed Lincoln the first time? Hmm?"

Cyclone lurched up from his chair and staggered backward.

"You can't be … are you suggesting ... for Christ sake, sir!"

"You owe me, young man. I did you a solid by giving you your soul. There could be nothing sweeter than an actor murdering the rail splitter rebooted, Lincoln 2.0, just as an actor killed the initial rollout beta version back in 1865. And you're just the man to do it, too: the fire breather who has all of the Red States in a lather to declare and maintain their independence. You'll be a hero to the South."

"You're insane. I won't do it. I draw the line."

"Do you? Son, you've already crossed every line that there is to be crossed. You're in my pocket." He wrote a check and handed it to Cyclone. "A little extra for your troubles," he said, as Cyclone stared at the sum.

"But they'll put me in jail!"

"Lawyers," Hoopengarner said. "Lawyers, guns and money. We'll prove you can't kill a dead man. There's no precedent for killing a man who has come back to life. Lincoln is legally dead, therefore you can't legally be held responsible for killing him."

Kandor gaped at the check.

"You're my drone, son. My dragonfly. Fly me."

CHAPTER TWO
TANNED, RESTED AND READY

On the same Wednesday that Alexander World intended to wish Amanda Clocker a happy birthday, Abraham Lincoln stood on the steps of the Lincoln Memorial before a vast throng on the Mall, the biggest assemblage ever in that location, far larger even than the secesh convocation of more than a year ago, when those in attendance had viewed Cyclone on massive screens upon which his moon face was Webcast from his faux bunker allegedly from somewhere in the desuetude of the Old Confederacy, but actually from a studio in Burbank, California. It was a brilliant, sunny day in late April. The cherry blossoms on the banks of the Potomac had bloomed, and the temperature had soared into the eighties. Streamers of red, white and blue bunting festooned every serviceable surface as a lanky black silhouette in a stovepipe hat plodded to a podium. Lincoln had foregone the red power ties and blue suits ("not my style") and returned to 19th-century attire. He was flanked by Secret Service agents. People thrust up signs: Abe 2016. He's tanned, rested and ready.

When Lincoln arrived at the speaker's stand, he doffed his stovepipe hat and from within it fished out a sheaf of papers, to much riotous laughter. No Teleprompter for this Ancient of Days. Moreover he had handwritten his speech, with a quill pen and ink drawn from a well. As the noon sun shone down on him like a playhouse spotlight,

Lincoln fumbled with his speech, the sheaf of papers rattling in his hands. A wind sprang up and nearly tore the pages loose from his grasp. Hanging on to them, Lincoln said into the microphone, his voice keening out over the throng: "I sure am glad I didn't lose these here papers. I got my Aqueduct bets written down on the back of 'em." Much laughter and applause.

In her Seattle office, Amanda Clocker was watching a live stream of the speech on her laptop when Alexander World entered without knocking and bearing gifts. He set two boxes with ribbons on top before her, one box larger than the first.

She looked at the boxes.

"What's the occasion, Alex?"

"Such a workaholic you've forgotten your own birthday, Amanda. But I didn't forget. Just as you didn't forget mine. Happy birthday to you!"

She looked at the boxes with dubiety and said: "You shouldn't have, Alex. Really." She was staring at the larger of the two boxes. She wondered: is that a ketchup stain at the bottom of it?

"Open this one first," he said, patting the smaller box. It too had red stains on it.

She stared at it.

"Open it, Amanda." The hairs on the nape of her neck stood up.

She slowly moved her eyes up to his. Then she looked quickly away from what was there, in those eyes. Or rather, what was no longer there. If ever it had been.

Her hands shook as she undid the bow and tore away the paper. She opened the box. Inside was a meat cleaver stained with dried blood.

Unable to tear her eyes away from it, she reached inside the box, gently removed the weapon and regarded it with dreamlike incredulity. The blood was crusty on the metal blade. At that moment, from the live stream, Abe was making his joke about his Aqueduct bets.

"A kitchen appliance, Amanda. One can't have too many Goddamned knives."

With a gesture almost of supplication, she gently lowered the blade cradled in her palms and gingerly set it down upon the table next to her laptop. In a dull voice, her eyes empty, she stared at the other, larger box and said, "What's in it, Alex?"

"It's a surprise, Amanda. Why don't you open it, and fucking find out?"

She looked up at him from her seat. He stood looking down at her.

"Open it, Amanda. You reap what you sow. Or should I say you download what you program?"

He had a dark, muddy look in his eyes. A shiver of terror ran through her.

She began to rise, but he planted his hands upon her shoulders and forced her back down into her chair. Boisterous applause from the live stream. Lincoln had said something witty. Amanda was staring at the bloodstains on the unopened box.

"Open it."

"Alex."

He tore apart the wrapping paper and yanked the lid off the box. The heads of his wife and heir were inside. They looked like decapitated bobble-head dolls. Their wide-staring eyes, plastic with deadness, regarded Amanda Clocker with accusatory Zombie-like malice.

"The trash wouldn't empty, Amanda," World said woodenly, beseechingly. His voice rose to an adolescent, resentful whine. He was back in his high-school computer cave, a skinny nerd with a pocket protector for his pens who wore big-rimmed glasses and was terrified of girls. "Why is that? Why?"

She began to scream but World clapped a hand over her mouth and as her eyes bulged up at him he said: "People mustn't hear, Amanda. Mustn't hear the truth. The truth that we ourselves make." She struggled desperately and tried to rise with his hand still clamped over her mouth. With his free hand he snatched up the meat cleaver and buried the blade into her liver, the liver of Prometheus. Blood jettisoned and stippled the computer screen, making Lincoln look as if he had been shot again. Her scream died in his hand, and then she died in his arms. World cradled her and crooned, "Happy Birthday to You," but substituted the world "Deathday" for "Birthday." He said, "My hard drive is corrupted, Amanda," and then he kissed her cold dead lips. "I'm Darkly Enlightened."

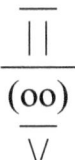

Within hours every single strand of the World Wide Web was aquiver with two astounding news stories vying for supremacy: Lincoln's speech and the arrest of Alexander World, who had been found wandering a Seattle street drenched in blood while grasping a meat cleaver and muttering over and over: DELETE. DELETE. DELETE. Along with a lot of other babble that made him sound like a pseudo-saint in the grip of a feverish religious delirium.

Lincoln's speech had poleaxed the pundits, who had devoted considerable energy to speculating in advance about what he might say. The whole world, it seemed, had been on tenterhooks, waiting for the first substantive utterances of this vatic voice from history. But his address was remarkably short, longer than the Gettysburg Address but shorter than his Second Inaugural Address. Lincoln told jokes, quite witty ones, which had his audience guffawing. At one point he turned back to look at his own marble statue and professed to be chagrined: "I believe that likeness makes me bigger than me breeches. I suppose a more fitting likeness for one such as I, would be me seated in an outhouse." Much laughter. The only substance of the speech was the disclosure that he intended to run an independent campaign under the banner of the Union Party, which was, he reminded the crowd, the name of the party for which he stood in the 1864 election, a fusion party that included the southern Democrat Andrew Johnson as the vice presidential candidate. Lincoln promised, however, that he would pick a different veep candidate "even if old Andy should happen to come back to life like I did." Not to disparage the former Tennessee governor, Lincoln smilingly recalled, "but the fact of the matter is, that bad boy got drunk on Inaggerashun Day back in '65 and they had to drag his ass, you'll pardon my French, off the reviewing stand and put him to bed. I do believe he emptied the contents of his stomach into a chamber pot." Much laughter and applause, as the cadaverous rail splitter towered over the throng while wearing a crooked watermelon-rind grin, his gray eyes dancing as usual with mischief and perhaps with some secret insight that he chose not to share. Short as the tall man's speech was, his humorous soliloquy was greeted with riotous applause and chants of "Abe! Abe! Abe!" as the former president reinstalled his stovepipe hat upon his head and concluded by saying, "I'll be tweetin' to y'all on Twitter. Stay online. Until then, ladies and gentleman, I must postpone further remarks. I beg your leave." A standing ovation. From somewhere a band cranked up "Hail to the Chief" and a party broke out during which three people were murdered and five women were raped.

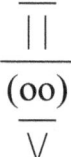

"There is no Abraham Lincoln," the man on the TV was saying. He was a French philosopher with an unpronounceable last name. "I'll go even further and say, "There never *was* an Abraham Lincoln."

It was a round table discussion about the Lincoln phenomenon. The moderator looked bemused. He was not as dumb as Trevor Credence on his Fox News POW! program, but he was, after all, a journo. His program was called WHAM!

"Explain," he said, addressing the philosopher by his last name and brutally mangling it. Hearing his name thus butchered, the philosopher offered an elitist grimace of disgust, making him look as if he were turning his nose up at plebeian cooking. He went on to condescend to the moderator: "There are no longer events, if ever there were such things. Can you grok that, sir? There are only pseudo-events. The Lincoln campaign is a pseudo-event, and Lincoln is a pseudo-Lincoln."

"Are you suggesting, sir, that he really is a Lincoln impersonator? What about the DNA match?"

"It doesn't matter whether he's really Lincoln or not," the philosopher said impatiently. "There never was a Lincoln, not even in the Civil War era. Lincoln, then and now, regardless of who this person actually is, is mythography, hagiography and historiography. He is the history of history. According to the pseudo-historian Delores Kearns Goodwin, Lincoln once told a visitor that he was 'clothed with immense power.' In reality he is clothed in the retrospective dreams, yearnings, ambitions and misunderstandings of the general public as distorted through the circus funhouse mirror-lens of the mass media and Daniel Day-Lewis. Lincoln, then and now, is an icon and not a man. However, although the general public does not understand this yet, history has come to an end. It's not because history has reached, as Fukuyama so erroneously argued, a teleological end point with the rise of globalization and the triumph of consumer capitalism — a claim demolished by the fall of the twin towers and the rise of Muslim extremism, though those too were pseudo-events — it is rather, that the very idea of historical progress has collapsed. And yet there is no dustbin in which to discard the remnants of the meta-narrative of America, because the very idea of the dustbin of history vanished along with the Marxists, who coined the term." The philosopher stopped talking then, and smiled superciliously. The moderator nodded with an expression of pseudo-profundity, as if he had understood a single thing that the French philosopher with the unpronounceable last name had just said. But he had not.

So it went. Another philosopher, a mystic steeped in Jung, contended that this Lincoln, or whoever he was, literally did not exist. He was, the second philosopher maintained, "a psychic projection of collective wish fulfillment, an archetype of the mass subconscious, a projection of the wounded World Soul, of the *Unus Mundus*." Two scientists, each of whom had shaggy gray eyebrows that they wagged in unified bemusement, listened to this bullshit with, well, bemusement. When their turn came, it became clear that they had no use for this sort of useless navel-gazing. They were hard-headed, hands-on men of action, empiricists who believed that only science offered answers, and that every other alleged way of knowing was sham and delusion, as useless as theology. The first scientist said that although DNA matches were reliable, it simply was not possible for anyone to rise from the dead. Hence, some big sham must be taking place. The second scientist vigorously disagreed, and offered his own model of the return of Lincoln: it involved negative entropy and quantum mechanics. He explained that although in a closed system all configurations of matter and energy naturally proceed from order to disorder, this phenomenon was merely statistical, representing the fact that there are so many more ways for a closed system to be disordered than to be ordered. Nevertheless, he explained, from time to time, by pure chance alone, disorder will mutate into order — wait long enough, he assured the moderator, who looked more confused than ever, and broken eggs will mend and a man will rise from the dead. This is what had happened with Lincoln, he said, adding that such incredibly quirky events can be expected from time to time under quantum mechanics as well, since QM shows that all successor states to prior states are merely probabilistic and not deterministic. Just as with thermodynamics, he finished up, QM showed that any event that can take place, no matter how unlikely, will take place if one waits long enough. He added, however, that Lincoln, like a "false vacuum" in quantum field theory, was metastable but actually unstable due to "instanton effects," which meant that at any moment Lincoln might be expected to tunnel to a lower (true) energy state: i.e., completely crumble into dust. The first scientist retorted that although what the second scientist said was all technically true, it was entirely misleading, because such events as eggs mending or a man rising from the grave were so unlikely that we should have to wait longer than the entire age of the universe so far to see even one such event happen. It did not help matters that the two scientists were conjoined twins, two heads on a single body. They became angry with each other, and began to butt heads. The moderator pleaded for order as the two heads viciously bonked away, eventually leaving the scientists too dazed to continue. The French philosopher remarked that the head-butting episode was yet another pseudo-event, and he denied that the conjoined twins existed except as a mass media model. He also brought up the recent shocking scandal involving Alexander World, who was cooling his heals in a madhouse while awaiting trial on murder charges. The French philosopher remarked that World's Dreamworlds were examples par excellence of pseudo-events, indeed they were entire pseudo-worlds, pseudo-histories, and with the collapse of World's business empire the long knives were already out. His business interests would be dismantled and competitors would buy or steal his source code, and World's Dreamworlds — his pseudo-worlds — would rapidly go viral, disseminated among the public at large, proliferating and eventually hijacking so-called real reality, a state of affairs he likened to the toppling of the Tower of Babel, because, he said, World's rivals would employ a Sumerian tongue as an incantation to disperse meaning and break down the ability of people to speak intelligibly to one another. He also explicated the short story "Tlön, Uqbar, Orbis Tertius" by Jorge Luis Borges, wherein an imaginary world invoked in a forged encyclopedia, a world founded on the principles of metaphysical idealism rather than metaphysical naturalism, gradually replaced the real world. Everyone associated the program wondered why they had staged it. It would have been wiser and more profitable to broadcast pro wrestling or the latest Twitter Trumpertantrum of Donald Trump, who was gradually losing his mind as Lincoln won primary after primary. The moderator looked exhausted, like someone who had just run a gantlet formed by a gang of faggot intellectuals who had pummeled him with resin bags of theory. Elvis Kandor — aka Cyclone — switched off the TV with his remote.

He was at home in the Burbank condo he shared with his spouse, John Caswell. The home had been bought with Homer Hickenlooper's money. He was taking a break for his busy Cyclone tour schedule, which was scheduled to resume next week with a swing through the Rocky Mountain States. The latest check that Hickenlooper had written him was on a table beside him. He heard the key turning in the door. Caswell came in.

"John, do you know what I am?"

"What are you, Elvis? Or who are you? Maybe that's the important question."

"I'm a pseudo-event, and a pseudo-man. Par excellence."

Caswell saw the check and his eyes got big.

"What in hell does that madman want you to do now?"

Kandor told him.

"We're getting out of here," Caswell said, panicked. Kandor had turned to his laptop, open and displaying his speaking schedule. Caswell closed the lid, grabbed his lover by the shoulders and yanked to him to his feet.

"The Cyclone tour is over, Elvis," Caswell said. "Forever."

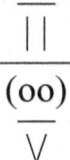

Back in sleepy Whitely, Idaho, Sam the bartender was watching the same round table discussion on the bar TV. He missed the Gang, but there were always new customers. As the two scientists bonked heads, Sam cleaned some beer mugs with a wet rag and meditated.

$$\frac{\overline{||}}{(oo)}$$
$$\overline{V}$$

CYCLONE GONE MISSING.

The splash headline, first flashed with a Breaking News banner on CNN, quickly went viral, along with the story over which the headline had been emblazoned. Within ten hours, the memescape was aboil and atwitter with the conviction that Cyclone had been kidnapped by agents of the Obama regime because the government wanted to silence this provocateur. Within two days this idea became a staple of Fox News commentary, though there was not a shred of evidence to support it. Within a week, the Obama regime's complicity in silencing the dreaded Cyclone was an undeniable pseudo-fact endorsed, according to hourly tracking polls, by upwards of eighty percent of the American public.

CHAPTER THREE
BEING AND NOTHINGNESS

"Son, do you know who I am?"

Shit Free or Die sat across from Homer Hickenlooper in the Pacific Heights flat shared by the Gang. There was a hole in the ceiling, made by a shotgun blast detonated by Shit Free just as Hoopengarner happened to be touring the property, as was his wont. The other gang members were out, but Becky the Bike, Shit Free's lover, sat with him on the sofa across from Hickenlooper, who had settled into an easy chair. Shit Free was drunk. Becky looked concerned. She clung to Shit Free in a proprietary way. She wore a clinging red mini-skirt and a halter-top bra with pointed cones. Her lips were scarlet with lipstick, and she smelled as if someone had smashed a bottle of cheap perfume over her head. She had on platform shoes and cheap fishnet stockings. She had just finished a stint working the Tenderloin, and some of the rolled-up money that she had earned made a green bouquet in the cleavage of her ample tits. Shit Free had hand-rolled a joint and now with a jaunty grin, which displayed his lack of upper front teeth but also the skulls painted on his lower teeth, he blew smoke up toward the hole in the ceiling and said, slurring his words: "No, poppy, I sure dunno who in hootin' hell you are, but you knocked on the door and I let ya in. Who in hell are ya?"

"My name is Homer Hickenlooper.

"Homo?"

"Homer. I own this property. Why'd you shoot a hole in the ceiling, son?"

Shit Free grinned luminously — he wore no shirt, but a black leather vest only, which showed off the tattoos on his muscular arms — and a wide-brimmed cowboy hat. Blue jeans and boots. He threw an arm around The Bike and drew her to his side. "My bitch and me, we wuz having a fight, that's all. This here's my bitch. Her name is Becky, but I call her The Bike, cuz I ride her. I shot a hole in the ceiling cuz I was pissed."

"What's your name, son?"

Shit Free told him. Hickenlooper looked impressed.

"Do you know, Shit Free," the magnate said, "that every person I meet, I turn to shit? It's my hobby."

"Well I'm Shit Free, poppy, so I guess that won't work with me."

"Like Medusa turned every person who looked upon her to stone, I turn every man who strays into my presence into a corrupted version of himself, which is to say a true version of himself. I've corrupted and destroyed Alexander World, for instance."

"Who's that?"

"You've never heard of Alexander World? Alexander the Great?"

"No."

"Don't you read the papers, son?"

"Reading is for pussies."

"Don't you watch TV?"

"I download porn on the Internet, poppy."

"Understood. I corrupted Cyclone, too, though now he's missing. And I had a job for him to do. Maybe you'd like to do it instead, son."

"Do what?"

"What do you think of this Lincoln impersonator

who is leading in all the polls to be elected president?"

Shit Free let loose a torrent of obscenities.

"How'd ya like to shoot him, son? I'll pay you well."

"How much?"

Hickenlooper named the sum.

"Deal."

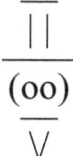

Donald Trump challenged Abe Lincoln to a wrasslin' match. Winner take all, loser drops out.

Lincoln accepted.

$$\frac{\overline{||}}{\underset{V}{(\text{oo})}}$$

Abraham Lincoln and Donald Trump met in the wrasslin' ring.

They met outdoors, in a special stadium hastily built in Rome, Georgia, and designed as an exact replica of the original Colosseum in the original Rome, before time and chance had reduced *Amphitheatrum Flavium* to partial but prestigious ruins. The new Colosseum, like the old, was clad in gleaming marble and held together with over 100,000 cubic meters of travertine stone which was set, not with mortar, but with three hundred tons of iron clamps. Trump had paid for this simulacrum out of his own pocket, betokening "the wonderful wall" he vowed to build on the southern border, a wall that would be paid for not by him but by Mexico or else by Little Marco Rubio or by somebody else.

However, in a concession to modernity, the New Colosseum was lined and ringed with vulgar, flashing neon lights and news tickers that updated onlookers with the latest important news of the day: primarily sports scores, celebrity sightings, gossip of every sort, and data about sex, murder, theft, fraud, embezzlement and the riveting plight of Alexander World, who had cut out Amanda Clocker's liver with a meat cleaver and then decapitated her and later carried her head around in the streets of Seattle as if he were a modern cephalophore, a headless saint who had suffered martyrdom by decapitation. The only point arguing against this interpretation was that World's own head was intact. Still, before the men in white coats threw their butterfly net around him, World threw his voice into Clocker's lips like a psychotic ventriloquist and through those dead lips he had spewed mad incantations that suggested a saint in the grip of vertiginous religious delirium, a saint who had been vouchsafed a glimpse of the ineffable, of *ein soph*, and who had jumped the shark and gone sailing over the edge because of it.

The bout between the two leading candidates for president was televised around the world, and streamed live on the Internet. The Goodyear blimp floated overhead. *Yuge* bets were placed. Famous announcers were in press boxes to describe the action and provide color commentary. This was bigger than the Super Bowl and the World Series combined. Many felt that in a physical contest between an ancient cadaver-cum-alive and a robust human orangutan with orange hair and a substantial penis, Trump had the edge. Alas, because most Americans have the attention span of a gnat, the memory of a goat, and sufficient comprehension ability only to wade (albeit laboriously) through a 140-character Twitter tweet, they did not know that Lincoln, in his youth, had participated in 300 wrasslin' matches and had lost only once. Or so legend has it. Certainly Trump didn't know this. The orange-haired sociopath didn't know *anything* — not even how to run a business, as attested by his bankruptcies.

Lincoln wore an ordinary white dress shirt with the sleeves rolled up to his elbows, shiny black pants held up by suspenders, and leather boots. Trump wore a sumo wrestler's silk *mawashi* with matching silk fronds. Essentially a gussied-up loin cloth, the *mawashi* bared his orange upper torso and his bandy orange legs. The loin cloth cradled Trump's huge, *yuge* basket, outlining in almost obscene detail that manhood swaddled within, a manhood that might ordinarily have made the mogul attractive to certain questing queers, according to certain sneering commentators, were Trump not a short-fingered vulgarian and a mental six-year-old who aspired to play with nuclear-tipped missiles as if they were radioactive Crayola crayons while wetting his pants and throwing apocalyptic Trumpertantrums in the White House.

It seemed now that only Lincoln could stand between Trump and the Oval Office in a Union quickly going kaput. Only Lincoln could stop Trump from plating the White House in 24-karat gold and slapping a *yuge* TRUMP PALACE sign on the front of it. Only Lincoln could stop Trump from converting the Washington Monument into high-rise condos for the nouveau-riche.

They wrassled.

After an initial inconclusive mixup, Trump shot down a hand and grabbed Lincoln's ankle in his boot. He yanked up that long leg and set the 16th president sprawling on his back on the blue mat set up in the faux Colosseum and cordoned off with gold ropes. A referee circled like a shark.

Trump could have flung himself atop a discombobulated Lincoln and pinned him on the spot. But that would have been too easy. Instead he had to boast a bit. With his tiny fists he beat on his massive chest like an aggrieved ape, like Mighty Joe Young dyed orange, and he bared his teeth. He let out a guttural roar and then grabbed his junk in his loin cloth and waggled it at Abe. "On your knees, Lincoln. On your knees! Say hi to the Family Jewels!"

"Say it, don't spray it," Lincoln replied.

By the time Trump was ready to pounce, Lincoln had sprung to his long legs with the athleticism and alacrity of a man about one-hundred-eighty-seven years younger than he actually was. He moved with the swiftness of a cat chasing a mouse. He got into a clinch with Trump, and then cunningly positioned himself so that the ref's view of Trump was momentarily blocked. In that fleeting moment Lincoln shot down a hand, seized Trump's balls in his loin cloth with an iron grip and then twisted then with all his might. Trump howled in agony and his eyes started out of his head. "Politics ain't beanbag, Mister," Lincoln leaned down and whispered urgently through gritted teeth while Trump shrieked. "You're in the real big leagues now. You ain't wrasslin' no more with Ted Cruz or Mario Rubio. You wrasslin' with *me*, boy. You wrasslin' with *history*." He let go of the mogul's manhood just as the ref circled around to get a good look at Trump. What he was saw was Trump sinking to his knees, listing to one side, and then falling over on his back while holding himself between the legs. His eyes were *yuge* and his lips quivered spasmodically, no sounds passing them but inarticulate grunts and moans. Little cartoon stars and squiggles representing addlement rose and swirled above Trump's head. Lincoln flung himself atop Trump and pinned his shoulders to the mat.

The ref fell to his hands and knees and began slapping his palm on the blue mat: "One … two … three!" A final slap of the hand. Fifty thousand voices roared as one from the stands.

"Kill Trump! Kill him," thousands yelled, giving the "thumbs down" gesture of ancient Roman gladiator fights, the Confederate battle flag wafting everywhere among the gibbering throng.

Lincoln grabbed a mic from a circling cameraman, gazed up at the crowed and then announced: "I'm the big buck of this lick. If any of you want to try it, come on and whet your horns." There were no takers. The confederate flags were meekly lowered.

Thus ended Donald Trump's presidential campaign

$$\frac{\overline{}}{\underset{\overline{}}{\underset{V}{(oo)}}}||$$

Long Abe Lincoln a little longer.

That was what the magazine cartoon had said, the words under a caricature of a beanpole Lincoln, back in 1864, after the man had been re-elected in a landslide.

Now Long Abe Lincoln doffed his stovepipe hat and ducked under the low transom of the office suite, telling his Secret Service agents to wait outside. They looked dubious, but complied with the request of the candidate of the Union Party. The date was September 10, 2016. The election was seven weeks away.

Lincoln straightened, his old bones audibly cracking, and towered purt near to the ceiling. He held the stovepipe hat in his left hand and with his right hand he fingered his watch chain. Once, when he had been on TV with Trevor Credence, the president had adopted modern dress. But he had returned to the lank black outfit of his previous tour of duty on this sad mortal coil, with his vest and bow tie and white shirt and his iconic hat. It polled well.

From Olympian heights he gazed down at the small, dowdy and seemingly insignificant man who stood up from his chair to greet Lincoln, and who extended his palsied hand. The 16th president of United States noted with bemusement the stray strands of hair atop the man's otherwise bald pate.

They looked like question marks.

"I'm Homer Hickenlooper, Mr. Lincoln," the real estate magnate said. Lincoln took his hand in greeting. "It's a pleasure to meet you, sir," Hickenlooper said. "In fact I'm in awe."

"Mr. Hickenlooper," Lincoln began with a preparatory drawl that seemed to betoken a story, "I learnt long ago that no man on earth merits a feeling of awe. Now perhaps Jesus will merit awe, if and when He ever returns. But so far after two whole millennia He still ain't shown up. So far as I am aware, He ain't never even sent anyone an e-mail." Lincoln laughed at his own bon mot, and Hickenlooper joined him in laughter. "Sit, sit," the magnate invited, gesturing at the chair on the other side of his desk. Lincoln awkwardly lowered his lank frame into the chair that was too small for him, and crossed one black-clad leg over the other. He set his stovepipe hat upon the upraised knee and looked at Hickenlooper and waited.

"Do you know, sir," Hickenlooper began, having not intended to say this, "that every man I meet, I corrupt? I make the pure impure."

Lincoln smiled lopsidedly.

"Do you have any idea, Mr. Lincoln, how much

money I've contributed to your campaign?"

"I've got a right general idea of it, sir, and I thank you kindly. It's why I made a point of dropping in to make your acquaintance while campaigning here in the Gold Rush city. Seemed the proper thing to do."

"You do understand, sir, that in modern American politics, you are a bought man. You speak of the Gold Rush City — an odd, very 19th-century locution for San Francisco. Let me remind you, Mr. Lincoln, of the Golden Rule: He who has the gold, makes the rules. When you are elected, as seems certain, you will do my bidding. Is that understood?"

Lincoln smiled and said nothing.

Hickenlooper became irritated. He rose to his feet, planted his hands on the desk and leaned toward the beanpole in the chair. The question-mark hairs atop his head boinged upward into exclamation points of indignation.

"This is what has been bothering me," he said, one hand still planted on the desk. With the other hand, he wagged a finger at Lincoln. "You're going to win this election, and you're not actually saying anything, about anything at all. Just like you're sitting there and smiling your smile, like someone sitting in the catbird seat, after I just got through telling you that I corrupt the innocent and that you're a bought man. That I own you. What in hell is your game, sir?"

"Game? I'm not generally a gamin' man, Mr. Hickenlooper, but I have taken a shine to bettin' on the horses with my good friend Sully Stark."

Hickenlooper slammed the flat of his hand on the desk and snarled, "Who in hell are you? Some C.I.A. plant? A false flag? History's greatest con artist? Speak, sir!"

"Why, I'm ol' Abe Lincoln, Mr. Hickenlooper. Same

as I ever was. I can scarcely imagine bein' someone other than who I am. If I were someone other than who I am, I wouldn't be who I am, would I?"

"Why are all your speeches nothing but jokes? And you have the people eating out of the palm of your hand! You're even ahead in the polls in the New Confederacy! You stand to win all fifty states! But what are you positions on the issues? What about the breakup of America? The second secesh? Note, sir, I am in favor of the breakup of the Union, and I expect, when you are elected again, that you will atone for your sin of starting the first Civil War by preventing the second Civil War and letting the Red States go in peace. Understand?"

"Mr. Hickenlooper, do you know what a politician is?"

"What a stupid question! Of course I know what a politician is. Who in hell doesn't know that?"

"A politician is a pragmatic man. And I'm a pragmatic man, sir. Always was. And I pragmatically perceive that the best way to win this election is just to be Abe Lincoln. I don't have to say what I stand for. I just have to be me. People won't vote for me because of my stands on the issues. They'll vote for me because I came back from the dead. I'm an icon who stepped out of the history books. The folks'll vote for me not because I'm a man, but because I'm a monument."

"But after you're elected, what in hell will you do? The New secession! Global warming! Muslim terrorists! Income inequality! The debt crisis! The Mideast morass! Overpopulation! Resource depletion! Conquest, War, Famine and Death! The Four Horsemen of the Apocalypse! The end is nigh! Speak, sir!"

"Some time ago, Mr. Hickenlooper, I bet on a pale horse named Death in the sixth race at Aqueduct. And do you know, it came in? It paid twelve dollars on a two dollar ticket."

Hickenlooper looked apoplectic.

"Do you have any idea how important I am, Mr. Lincoln?"

"I've a right general idea that you *think* you're important."

"I, sir, am a man of aplomb. Quick-witted, cheeky and self-possessed, except when I pretend to be otherwise for strategic benefit. Do you understand me?"

"Well there was a party once, Mr. Hickenlooper, which was composed of ladies and gentlemen. A fine table was set and the people were greatly enjoying themselves. Among the crowd was one of those men who had audacity — was quick-witted, cheeky and self-possessed — never off his guard on any occasion. After the men and women had enjoyed themselves by dancing, promenading, flirting, etc., they were told that the table was set. The man of audacity — quick-witted, self-possessed and equal to all occasions — was put at the head of the table to carve the turkeys, chickens and pigs. The men and women surrounded the table, and the audacious man being chosen carver whetted his great carving knife with the steel and got down to business and commenced carving the turkey, but he expended too much force and let a fart — a loud fart so that all the people heard it distinctly. As a matter of course it shocked all terribly. A deep silence reigned. However the audacious man was cool and entirely self-possessed; he was curiously and keenly watched by those who knew him well, they suspecting that he would recover in the end and acquit himself with glory. The man, with a kind of sublime audacity, pulled off his coat, rolled up his sleeves, put his coat deliberately on a chair, spat on his hands, took his position at the head of the table, picked up the carving knife and whetted it again, never cracking a smile nor moving a muscle of his face. It now became a wonder in the minds of all the men and women how the fellow was to get out of his dilemma. He squared himself and said loudly and distinctly: 'Now, by God, I'll see if I can't cut up this turkey without farting!'"

"Get out."

After Lincoln left, Hickenlooper contacted Shit Free by cellphone. "Shoot him," Hickenlooper said.

Shit Free shot Lincoln.

Or rather, he shot Lincoln's stovepipe hat. Which was almost the same thing.

But not quite.

The hat flew into the air and cartwheeled.

It came down, brim first, into Lincoln's outstretched hands. He examined the bullet hole in it while the Secret Service agents went apeshit.

"Same thing happened to me in eighteen hundred and sixty three," Lincoln drawled aloud, recalling a little-known attempt on his life while he had been riding alone on horseback to the White House from his summer retreat. Someone had shot at him from a tree limb and put a hole through his stovepipe hat, which had then as now flown off his head. A moment later Lincoln was wrestled to the sidewalk and covered in a black-clad cloud of paid defenders. Pandemonium broke out among a throng of onlookers on Market Street. Within minutes tweets on Twitter blamed the Muslims. The shooter, one tweeter solemnly averred, "had a big schnoz," meaning that he was Arab. A cascade of comments, many of which were strategically hashtagged, called for nuking all Muslim nations. In trying to kill America's greatest icon, it was said with rage, the Muslims were trying to kill America itself.

In fact, no one had seen the would-be assassin, because Shit Free had fired from the sixth floor of an abandoned office tower across Market Street from Hickenlooper's San Francisco offices. The tower, owned by Hickenlooper, was slated to be razed and replaced with luxury condos catering to dot-com cruds. Shit Free was, as he had repeatedly assured the magnate, a perfect shot. But as he pulled the trigger he was also drunk, and owing to this fact and perhaps also because he was not very bright, Shit Free had assumed that Lincoln's famous stovepipe hat was actually part of his anatomy. In fact as the hat cartwheeled into the air and Secret Service agents converged on Lincoln, Shit Free cracked a skull-toothed grin and pumped a fist, convinced that he had done his job. He then put the rifle into a box, tied it with wrapping paper and withdrew into the darkened corridors of the empty building, only to make his escape minutes later through a rear service entry door that opened on an alley. Shit Free quickly blended in with the pedestrian traffic of San Francisco.

He would have made good his escape, too, were it not for the fact that recently, President Obama, in a show of strength meant to reassure the fracturing union, had ordered drone overnights of all major American cities. San Francisco was under twenty-four hour surveillance from Eyes in the Sky, and one such eye snapped a perfect picture of Shit Free's face in the window, squinting into the gunsights. It caught the flash of fire from the muzzle, and this intelligence was instantly conveyed to C.I.A. headquarters in Langley, Virginia. By various strategies that shall remain secret, because, after all, the government must have secrets from the people it allegedly serves, Shit Free's mug was quickly matched with a name. Within hours a SWAT team was converging on the Pacific Heights flat shared by the Gang.

Although politically at odds, the Gang constituted a Band of Brothers, with an all-for-one, one-for-all mentality. And they all hated the government, albeit for different reasons. Moreover, each of them was heavily armed except of course for Becky the Bike, who was not allowed to handle firearms because she was a girl and technically because she was not a "brother." As the sun fell and the San Francisco fog moved in like smoke from a distant battlefield, turning the violet sky gunmetal gray, a firefight broke out. Police lights strobed the gloom, and concussion bombs were hurled into the house. There were explosions, and a fire broke out. The SWAT team charged the premises and within minutes it dragged out the Gang, several of whom were wounded, including Shit Free, but none were dead.

Watching live TV coverage of the standoff, Homer Hickenlooper realized that his dreams of either buying Lincoln off or stopping his return to the Oval Office had just died in the twilit fires in Pacific Heights. And with this had died his dreams of a New Confederacy. Lincoln was leading in the polls everywhere, including the Deep South, under the sway of the Evangelicals who had linked him to Christ. The president had been right: the people might not vote for Lincoln the man, especially if they knew what policies he intended to pursue. But they were not planning to vote for the Man. They intended to vote for the Monument.

Alone in his office, the lights dimmed, the glow of the TV showing the fires in Pacific Heights, Hickenlooper contemplated his next move. He wondered what crazed, egotistical impulse had spurred him to recruit a drunken retard named Shit Free or Die to shoot Lincoln, to carry out the charge that he had originally given to Cyclone, who had mysteriously vanished. He did not feel he could count on Shit Free's silence, now that he was in custody. For years, Hickenlooper had deftly evaded justice, leaving behind a trail of bodies on the way. Now, nearing the end of his life, he deemed it likely that his luck had run out. It was, he reflected, a good thing that he had taken out an insurance policy against this eventuality.

He put on his DreamGlass and settled back into his chair with a smile, twining his fingers across his pumping heart, still going strong after lo these many years.

It was 1965. He was young again. The world was his oyster. He was living in the America he had always dreamed of. Barry Goldwater was president.

He left his office and took the elevator down to Market Street. It was daylight. He was thunderstruck to discover that everyone was running down the street, panic in their faces. It was a stampeding mob, utter pandemonium. At first he heard nothing, and with a terrified start he wondered whether he lost his hearing. But then the audio switched on. Screams rent the sky. Hickenlooper shouldered his way slantwise across the mob running down the street and found a news rack with the San Francisco Chronicle in it. President Goldwater's severe mug, adorned with his trademark horn-rimmed glasses, like an abstract American eagle squatting on the bridge of his nose with wings extended, was plastered across the front page. FINAL SOLUTION jumped out from the terrifyingly large headline. SOVIETS. VIETNAM. Dazed, Hickenlooper dropped a quarter into the box and opened it. Change was spat back. Back then, the daily newspaper was just a dime. He looked first at the date: August 4, 1965. EXTRA EXTRA EXTRA. Just as he was reading the FINAL SOLUTION headline, the sky went white and a piercing whine assailed his eardrums, which popped. Then white went black, and

Hickenlooper heard and saw nothing again as towering mushroom clouds bloomed over the greater Bay Area. A parting gift, a little tweak, a virus in virtuality, courtesy of the devilish Amanda Clocker, who of course had recently encountered her own unexpected tweak, finishing up with a meat cleaver downloaded into the liver of Prometheus. When the police came they found Hickenlooper draped across his desk, his DreamGlass shades still affixed to his forehead. They righted him in his chair and tore the glasses off of his face. His expression was contorted with horror, his eyes bulging in their sockets. He was dead. The coroner ruled it a heart attack. Curiously, they later found traces of radiation on him. In fact, the Geiger counter needles jumped off the charts.

$$\frac{\overline{||}}{(oo)}$$
$$\overline{V}$$

Lincoln was elected president in a landslide.

$$\frac{\overline{||}}{(oo)}$$
$$\overline{V}$$

Elvis Kandor — aka Cyclone — missed the stage.

After learning that Homer Hickenlooper had hired Kandor to assassinate Lincoln, his spouse, John Caswell, had hustled Kandor out of town and into hiding. They went to New York City, where they stayed with friends. There, Kandor "got off the junk," as Caswell put it. Cold turkey. No more Cyclone, no more Hickenlooper, no more tours, no more Webcasts, no more acting. Nothing. Cyberspace was abuzz with his disappearance, which of course was attributed to the machinations of the Obama regime, or to Muslim terrorists, or else to space aliens. No theory, no matter how outlandish or half-baked, failed to be accepted on the Web. Indeed the zanier the hypothesis, the more currency it gained.

Under the watchful and protective influence of Caswell and their friends in New York City, Kandor decompressed. He went through the typical withdrawals of an addict going cold turkey, but he seemed to be getting better. He hid in plain sight, no one recognizing his familiar moon face in the mobs coursing through the concrete canyons like lab rats in the world's biggest maze. He and Caswell and their friends attended the Metropolitan Opera (where they saw the Ring Cycle) and a Rothko exhibition at MOMA. They dined at pleasant if pricey restaurants in the Village, and they visited the 9/11 memorial at Ground Zero. The election came and went, and one day Kandor disappeared. His destination was Washington, D.C. He did not tell anyone that recently, his identity had changed again, though he was still an actor.

He was John Wilkes Booth.

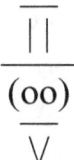

On the day after Lincoln's landslide election, Paradise 72 released a video of the alleged Lincoln corpse, still crucified on a cross, suspended like a scarecrow over, not a field, but a yellow desert under a blue sky. A jihadist had mounted a ladder and held a dagger to the throat of the corpse. Speaking in flawless, British-accented English, the hooded jihadist said: "On your infidel Inauguration Day, January 20, 2017, unless the ransom we have demanded is paid in return for releasing this corpse into infidel hands, we shall behead Lincoln. In so doing we shall destroy not just America's iconic infidel symbol, but America itself."

$$\frac{\overline{||}}{\frac{(oo)}{\overline{V}}}$$

On January 14, 2017, the night before President-elect Abraham Lincoln was to leave his Springfield home to fly to Washington preparatory to his inauguration, the long shadow of a lank man topped by a stovepipe hat loomed along a tall wall in a full moon. It was a surprisingly mild evening for January in Springfield.

Uncharacteristically, Rob Boyle, the jumpy Springfield cop attached to the Lincoln guard, had fallen asleep. He jerked awake from the middle of a dream.

He recalled it vividly, and for a moment he felt certain that he was still in it. Seeing the shadow moving along the wall, he snatched his gun from its holster, sprang to his feet and dropped into a defensive crouch. He pointed the gun at the shadow. The gun quivered in his hand as he shook all over, dumbstruck with terror.

In his dream, he had been cruising by himself through downtown Springfield, at the wheel and in charge at last, unencumbered by a partner. He was the good guy, riding the tiger of his car. He did not know that those who ride the tiger, sometimes end up inside.

He slowed his squad car because ahead of him, two black teenagers were strolling down the center of the road.

Jaywalkers!

One of the black teenagers was enormous, almost inhuman! He must have been almost seven feet tall, weighing more than three hundred pounds. He was dressed baggily, in hip-hop attire: Cargo shorts that fell below his knees, yellow socks, designer sneakers that he probably stole. A baggy black T-shirt.

Officer Boyle slowed the car to a crawl, rolled down his window, propped an elbow atop the door and yelled out at the two black punks: "Get off the road and onto the sidewalk, boys. You're jaywalking!"

The enormous gorilla of a black boy looked back over his shoulder at Boyle and proffered a menacing simian stare.

The two teens sauntered only slowly back toward the sidewalk. Infuriated by such dilatory behavior, Officer Boyle parked the car and began opening the door, hand on his gun.

The big black boy again looked back over his shoulder, and his dark muddy pupils set in their balls of white met the eyes of Boyle. Boyle's gun was out of its holster and the black boy saw it.

With a quick and surprisingly agile whirl for someone so large, the black boy hurled a handful of cigars at Boyle. A couple of them struck him in the face.

The dream got vague after that, a blur of flying limbs and sunlight shattered into splinters by the leaves of trees overhead. The boy seemed to have his hands up in surrender or, alternatively, he had thrown them upward in rage and was running in a dead sprint toward Boyle and bellowing, as if to tackle the officer. Alternatively, he was running away. Either way, a moment later the gun was firing, bucking in Boyle's hands and spitting shot. The gun cracks were deafening to the officer, and he saw blazes of fire and smelled gunpowder. It was as if the gun were shooting itself and he were merely holding on to it, going for a wild ride like a man atop a runaway horse without reins. There was a high ringing sound in his ears, and the blood rushed to his temples. The veins in his forehead pounded, pounded. A moment later the enormous black body was splayed across a green lawn, bleeding from the head, and people, all of them black, were darting out of their houses and sprinting toward the prone form on the lawn. Some of them were holding cellphones and recording the scene for posterity. Panicked, Boyle wildly pointed the gun around, first at this person and then at another, and that was when he woke up and saw the shadow on the wall in the silvery moonlight and now he was pointing his gun at that shadow.

He felt a heavy hand upon his shoulder, and shuddered. He lowered the gun, and sat back down on his folding chair. Lincoln then sat down next to him, awkwardly arranging his long lank form on a wall ledge.

Boyle pointed the gun at the ground, but kept his hands wrapped tightly around the handle. In the moonlight, Lincoln's eyes were sunk in black shadows that made them look not like eyes but like the sockets of a skull. The president-elect grinned lopsidedly, the tawny leather of his face nearly white in the strong moonlight. The president composed his hands on his knees and seemed to stare in an evaluating way at Boyle, whose eyes met Lincoln's eyes, those black skull sockets, for a long and terrible moment. Then Boyle lowered his eyes and fondled his gun barrel. He felt the skin rise on the nape of his neck.

"Well, young man," Lincoln began with a lazy drawl, as if preparatory to a story, perhaps a funny one, "when I was first elected back in eighteen hundred and sixty and the nation was falling apart, I was terribly afraid.

I didn't know if I was up to the job."

Boyle listened in sullen silence.

"As time and the Civil War went on, young man, I became convinced that I was the instrument of Divine Providence. A heady thought."

Boyle waited for more.

"The instrument of Destiny," Lincoln went on in a dreamy, speculative tone of voice. "Both sides in the war prayed to the same God, yet the prayers of neither side were fully answered. And the war went on."

Boyle watched the ground. Then he heard a crunch. His head shot up.

Lincoln was eating an apple.

The cop watched, fascinated, as the sixteenth president devoured the apple in four quick bites and then pitched the core to the ground. "And now I'm back, unbidden of my own free will, and elected again. To finish, perhaps, what I started, but was deprived of bringing to an auspicious conclusion. First I was to win the war, which I did. But then I was to bind up the nation's wounds, especially its racial wounds. However, an actor's bullet deprived me of that opportunity."

Lincoln paused, sighed, and then looked off into middle distance, saying nothing for long moments. Boyle found himself staring at Lincoln's long, weathered, bony hands, which were composed between his knees. Those long fingers.

"Who could but fail to believe that Divine Providence is setting matters aright by bringing me back?" Lincoln said.

"You believe that?" Boyle asked, watching the hands, the fingers now intermingling and forming a cat's cradle.

"Perhaps astonishingly, the answer is No. It is

tempting to believe, but the better part of experience and wisdom has taught me to believe just the opposite."

Boyle watched the fingers. Lincoln disentangled them and one of the hands drifted down toward his boots, beside which, upon the mud, he had placed his stovepipe hat. He plucked up the hat, placed it upon his head, looked off into some ethereal vision of the distant past and recited from memory: "Happy day, when, all appetites controlled, all poisons subdued, all matter subjected, mind, all conquering mind, shall live and move as the monarch of the world. Glorious consummation! Hail fall of Fury! Reign of Reason, all hail!"

"What?"

Lincoln shrugged. "From an old speech of mine, delivered when I was just thirty-three years of age. It was about temperance, believe it or not. I was young and stupid, to say that."

"Cut the bullpucky, sir. Who are you, really? What in hell are you?"

"I am Chaos," Lincoln said immediately and sharply, voice somber. "I'm contingency. I'm the joker in the deck, the spanner in the works. History's bewhiskered troll. There is no rhyme or reason for my being back here, just as there was no rhyme or reason for my being president during the Civil War. It was a happy accident — or unhappy, as some might believe. Including you." Lincoln reached forward and patted Boyle on the knee. The latter stiffened at the touch and sight of that enormous, wrinkled, long-fingered hand with its bony knuckles going up and down on his knee. He clung fiercely to the gun and heard Lincoln say: "There's no reason for anything, just accidents, monstrous moments now and then leavened by happy accidents. No good, no evil, just the slow, pitiless, indifferent tick of the clock of History, the vast Cosmos indifferent to all our schemes and dreams. History is a whore, young man. You pay it with meaning of your own making, and it will fuck you blind in gratitude."

Boyle watched, mesmerized, as the large, leathery hand rose from his knee, and approached his head. He flinched and then stiffened as with those long, bony fingers, Lincoln lightly ruffled Boyle's hair.

"Young man," Lincoln drawled in a near-whisper, florid lips puckering slightly, "You do so remind me, physically, of Joshua Speed, my good friend with whom, for many years, I shared a bed, in the days when both of us were ... unwed." Lincoln drew near, very near. Boyle could smell him. He smelled of sweat and bootblack and history and dust. He smelled of the grave.

Lincoln rose, and his shadow leaned forward. His boots soles crunched on gravel.

In his dream a mob attacked Boyle. "You killed that young man," they were screaming. "You killed him." They were upon him, and a struggle ensued. Someone snatched his gun and it went off. Boyle saw a blinding flash of light, and his ears rang. The sky whirled above him. The sunlight flickered down through the revolving tree leaves and that was the last thing that he saw except for the moonlight shining down, for day had suddenly turned to night. He was flat on his back, looking up at the star-spangled sky. He still held the gun. Smoke curled out of its barrel. He closed his eyes. Blood flowed from his ears.

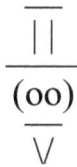

President-elect   Abraham   Lincoln   and   Vice

President-elect Sullivan Stark arrived in Washington, D.C., on January 15, 2017, five days before the Inauguration.

Stark had been thunderstruck at Lincoln's offer of the vice presidency on the Union Party ticket, and at first he had demurred. But Lincoln told him that there was no one in the 21st century whom he trusted more than Stark. The latter gradually warmed to the idea as he reviewed the banal events of his life, his lusterless decades as a cop in Springfield, where he had never shot anyone nor had been shot at nor had saved anyone's life. He wasn't the cop who had seen it all. He was the cop who *hadn't* seen it all. He was the man who had written a lot of traffic tickets and had once saved a cat trapped in a tree Now, late in life, and with the recent death of his beloved Hortense weighing heavily on his mind, he had accepted Lincoln's offer. He had no idea what Lincoln intended to do as president, any more than anyone else had. After the election, Lincoln confided to Stark that he would reveal his true intentions in his Inaugural Address. The president-elect labored over draft after draft of the speech, alone in a study, employing not modern computer technology but a lonely quill pen dipped in a humble jar of ink. Scratch, scratch, scratch, the quill tip running over the sheaf of papers night after night, the address written and rewritten. Cross out this line, insert that line. There he was, hunched over The Speech under a spare light, wire-rimmed glasses sliding down the prominent nose, the stems looping around the elephantine ears. Lincoln showed The Speech to no one, not even Stark. But everyone understood that these utterances would change everything. The world held its breath as the clock ticked to noon on Inauguration Day.

That day began sunny and bright, but ominous clouds moved in as the Lincoln cavalcade arrived. Stark was preoccupied, thinking not only of what lay ahead, but also about the mysterious death of Boyle, which had been ruled a suicide. Abe was dressed in his old finery, the stovepipe hat (with the bullet hole in it) et al. He sat in the limo with President Obama, whom Lincoln had met for the first time that morning during a White House reception. Obama had sobbingly confessed to Lincoln about the Spock ears. The president-elect in turn had complimented "a man of your color" for attaining the land's highest office. Then the president-elect whacked the outgoing chief executive on the knee and told a risqué joke that embarrassed everyone in the room, including the president and his wife and two daughters. But Lincoln laughed like a hyena, his high-pitched hilarity the only sound in a room otherwise frozen in shocked silence.

Lincoln's stovepipe hat bobbed above the vast throng gathered around the Capitol as he and Stark made their way to the podium where within minutes they would be sworn in. A voice shrilled from the crowd, *"Sic semper tyrannis!"* Stark saw the pistol even before the Secret Service agents did. He seized Lincoln, hurled him to the steps upon which they were striding and covered Lincoln's body with his own. The bullet whizzed harmlessly overhead, hitting no one but striking a tree branch, and the crowd set upon the shooter. The man who regretted his life realized that he had just saved Abraham Lincoln's life. He was a hero of history.

Police and Secret Service agents rescued Elvis Kandor from the crowd, which was beating him, and hustled the hapless failed actor and failed assassin to his fate. After a brief consultation, all agreed that the swearing-in should proceed on schedule, which it did.

After Lincoln took the oath, he approached the podium, emblazoned with the seal of the president of the United States. A hush fell over the crowd. What would he say? What *could* he say?

Watching the events unfold on his TV from his bar in Whitely, Idaho, Samuel Beckett cleaned a beer mug with a wet rag and muttered: "They're all waiting for Godot. But Godot won't show. Godot *can't* show."

Lightning forked. Thunder rumbled, and the Washington Monument quivered like a tuning fork. Big, glossy drops of rain pelted the crowd, and then the skies opened and a downpour ensued. Undaunted, Lincoln, who had removed his stovepipe hat, put it back on again to shield himself against the rain, and rattled the sheaf of papers in his hands. Already they were soggy. The rain sluiced off the wide brim of his black hat as his reedy voice keened out over the crowd: "Dear America," he began. Then another bolt of lighting cleaved the sky and lunged downward toward Lincoln, striking the top of his stovepipe hat like the white-hot finger of God. The hat jumped off his head.

At that moment, half a world away, the P/72 jihadists beheaded the Lincoln corpse and streamed the event live on the World Wide Web.

Back in Washington, thunder gonged. Before the eyes of all assembled in Washington and billions more worldwide on TV and the Internet, the new and old president crumbled to dust just as his severed head rolled onto the desert sand half a world away. All that was left in Washington was his skull, the stovepipe hat aslant atop it, perched on a pile of black ashes that steamed in the rain. His other skull lay in the Levant dust. The pages of his speech, the speech that would change everything, were swept up in a howling wind and scattered among the crowd like failed lottery tickets. Lighting again forked overhead and the downpour became torrential.

Avid hands snatched at those wafting pages, which

began spiraling downward like assassinated butterflies. The ink ran in the rain and the pages, when they floated to earth, curled in the mud. Everyone tried to read them, but they were blank. They wept ink.

Thus did Sullivan (Sully) Stark, a plain and unprepossessing man, much like the original version of Lincoln himself, mount the throne of destiny late in life, belying his banal and heretofore failed fate that he once had in common with those nameless and numberless nonentities plodding pathetically toward the good grave. As the only character in this absurd and (let's be frank) rather idiotic jape to meet a good or at least acceptable outcome, it behooves us now to consider his presidency in a new time of crisis, and to reflect on the hazards of time, fate and destiny.

But that is for a sequel, which, fortunately, shall never be written, unless it is.

THE END